EGYPTIAN CHRONICLES

THE SPITTING COBRA

Hopi and Isis can remember the terrible accident on the River Nile, when they lost their parents to crocodiles. Hopi still bears crocodile teethmarks on his leg. But five years have passed, and they've been lucky: eleven-year-old Isis is a beautiful dancer, and she's been spotted by a dance and music troupe in the town of Waset. Now they live with the troupe, and Isis performs regularly. Meanwhile, thirteen-year-old Hopi, marked by the gods, pursues his strange connection with dangerous creatures . . .

Join them in the world of ancient Egypt as they uncover the dark deeds happening around them. If there's anything you don't understand, you may find an explanation at the back of the book.

Also by Gill Harvey

Egyptian Chronicles series
The Horned Viper

Coming soon
The Sacred Scarab
The Deathstalker

Also available
Orphan of the Sun

EGYPTIAN CHRONICLES

THE SPITTING COBRA

GILL HARVEY

BLOOMSBURY

LONDON BERLIN NEW YORK

Bloomsbury Publishing, London, Berlin and New York

First published in Great Britain in 2009 by Bloomsbury Publishing Plc
36 Soho Square, London, W1D 3QY

A CIP catalogue record of this book is available from the British Library

ISBN 978 0 7475 9563 2

The paper this book is printed on is certified independently in accordance
with the rules of the FSC. It is ancient-forest friendly.
The printer holds chain of custody.

Typeset by Dorchester Typesetting Group Ltd
Printed in Great Britain by Clays Ltd, St Ives plc

1 3 5 7 9 10 8 6 4 2

www.bloomsbury.com/childrens
www.bloomsbury.com/gillharvey

For Kijana

CONTENTS

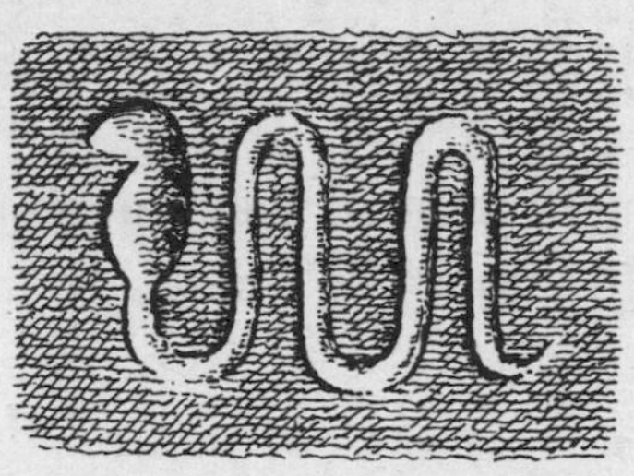

PROLOGUE

In the flickering light of the oil lamp, the gold on the lid of the casket gave off a fiery glow. Nakht turned the precious object over in his hands, examining it closely. He opened the lid and peered inside; he ran his finger over the fine inlaid patterns of carnelian, lapis lazuli and gold.

'A very fine copy, don't you think?' asked Baki.

Nakht shook his head. 'This is no copy. I'd know it anywhere,' he said. 'I worked on it myself. And I placed it in the tomb with my own hands.'

Baki stroked his chin. 'You're sure?'

'By Horus and all the gods, I couldn't be more certain.'

Baki gave a heavy sigh. 'Then let us await the messenger.'

The two foremen lapsed into silence. Nakht placed

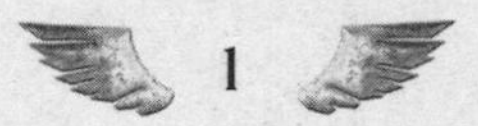

the casket on the floor, and they gazed at it, as though it might be able to give them an answer to the mystery.

At last, there was a soft knock on the door. Nakht stood, and went to open it. A young man stepped inside, still breathless from running down the mountain.

'Well?' demanded Baki. 'What did you find?'

'The tomb has not been touched, sir,' replied the young man. 'The door is still in place, with the seals of the Great Place in perfect condition.'

Nakht sat down heavily, shaking his head. 'Impossible,' he murmured.

'You're sure you checked the right tomb?' queried Baki.

'Of course, sir,' said the messenger. 'I checked three times, and all the tombs nearby, just to be sure.'

The two foremen exchanged glances. The young man stood nervously, shifting from one foot to the other.

'You may go,' said Baki.

'Thank you, sir.' The messenger stepped quickly to the door, and disappeared into the night.

Nakht stood up again, and started pacing the room. 'So,' he said. 'This casket has been found in our village, but it belongs in a royal tomb. This much is sure. But the robbers are cunning. They did not break into the tomb via the doorway. They must have made another way in. It all points to one thing, Baki. The robbers live among us, here in Set Maat. No one else knows the mountain so well; no one else has the knowledge and skill to create another entrance.'

Baki ran a hand over his head, then once more stroked his jaw. 'This cannot be,' he muttered. 'I cannot believe that such a terrible thing has come among us.'

'There is no other explanation,' said Nakht, his face full of sorrow. 'We cannot hide from the truth. We must find the robbers, even if they are our relatives and friends. It is our sacred duty.'

'But how?'

Nakht sat down, rested his elbows on his knees and bowed his head. 'Yes, how,' he murmured.

The two men were not afraid of silence. They had known each other for many, many years. They sat and stared at the beautiful casket once more, each wondering whether the other would come up with an idea. At last, it was Nakht who spoke.

'The harvest approaches,' he said. 'Let us each throw a party. We can afford to be generous; let there be music and dancing and rich food and wine. Indeed, we must make sure the wine flows freely, for that is our key. Wine and good cheer encourage tongues to speak freely. Someone will say something that should have remained a secret.'

Baki smiled wryly. 'I am surprised at you, brother,' he said. 'I never thought I would live to see you encourage drinking and revelry.'

But Nakht remained serious. 'Perhaps so,' he said. 'But I never thought I would live to see such things happen in our midst. Do you think it a good idea?'

Baki spread his hands expressively, and shrugged. 'I can see nothing wrong with it,' he said. 'And vanity may play a part as much as flagons of wine. If a robber's wife has acquired sumptuous jewellery, she may be tempted to wear it.'

'Then let us go ahead. The sooner the better.'

'Well . . .' Baki frowned. 'It may not be so easy. There are a few problems.'

'Such as?'

'Our best music troupe cannot perform at the moment. Wab and her family have a sickness, and their finest young dancer has broken her arm.'

Nakht slapped his thigh impatiently. 'But there are others!'

'They are priestesses, brother,' Baki pointed out. 'Can we really call on them for such a purpose?' He paused. 'Perhaps it would be better to wait awhile.'

'No.' Nakht was determined. 'We have to carry out our plan now. Rumours are already spreading. If we cannot use our own troupe, we can hire another. Let us send messengers to Waset; there are plenty of performers there. I will pay for them out of my own pocket if I have to.'

Baki could find no other objections. He nodded slowly. 'You speak wisely,' he said. 'We cannot delay. Let us send messengers first thing tomorrow.'

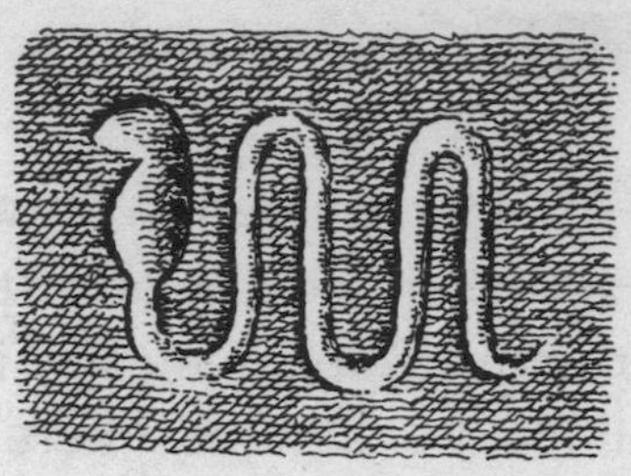

CHAPTER ONE

The woman was hysterical. With a trembling finger, she pointed to the corner of the storeroom, where the water jars were kept. Hopi approached quietly, and peered behind them. A snake lay coiled there, perfectly still.

Hopi recognised its blotchy brown and orange markings at once. 'It's not dangerous,' he said. 'If you leave it alone, it won't bite you. And even if it did, you would live.'

'I don't care!' the woman shrieked. 'I don't want that thing in my house!'

'It's only interested in mice,' Hopi pointed out. 'The mice that eat your stores of grain . . .'

The woman shook her head. 'Kill it! Just get rid of it!'

Hopi sighed. 'I'll take it away.'

Carefully, he moved one of the water jars so that the snake was in full view. Then, with a flick of his stick, he reached underneath and whipped it into a round papyrus basket. He fitted a lid on top and put the basket into a linen bag, which he slung over his shoulder.

'Now get it out of here,' the woman demanded.

Hopi looked at her calmly. 'It's harmless,' he told her. 'But as you fear it so much, perhaps you could offer some thanks.'

The woman frowned, and muttered under her breath. She reached for a wooden box by the doorway and rummaged inside.

'Here,' she said. 'Take this. It's a lucky amulet. I suppose a cripple needs all the luck he can get.'

Hopi felt stung. This woman was cruel, and not only to snakes. He took the charm and put it into his bag. 'Thank you, madam,' he said quietly.

He set off out of the house and up the street, trying his best not to limp. But the woman was right. He *was* a cripple. He would never be able to run and walk the way he once had. He was thirteen now. Five years ago, when he was eight, there had been a day that had scarred him for ever. It had left him and his sister Isis without parents, and had given him a terrible wound on his right leg. It had healed, slowly. But the marks would never fade, and the leg would always be weak.

As he made his way along the narrow, higgledy-piggledy streets of Waset, younger children recognised him and ran up, tugging his arm.

'Hopi! Hopi!' they cried. 'What have you caught? Is it a scorpion?'

Hopi shook his head.

'A lizard!' shouted the children. 'A snake!'

'Maybe.' Hopi couldn't help but smile.

'Can we see it?'

'Not this time. Sorry.'

'Oh please, please!'

Hopi gently pulled his arm free. 'Not today,' he said. 'This snake needs some peace.' And leaving the children behind, he headed out into the fields.

The music troupe's big costume box was almost empty. Pretty bracelets, collared necklaces, anklets and wigs lay neatly on the floor, and linen gowns were stacked in a pile. Mut and Isis had spent all morning sorting them out, and now Mut bent over the box to fish out the last few items.

'We've nearly finished,' she said. She held up a beautiful collar made of row after row of blue beads, with the occasional row of red. 'This is one of Mother's favourites. Oh – wait a minute. Something's tangled up in it.'

Isis looked up from teasing a knot out of a long black wig. 'That's my cowrie waistband!' she exclaimed. 'I'll wear that for the parties in Set Maat.'

Mut examined the waistband. 'I don't think it's yours,' she said. 'I think it's one of mine.'

'Let's see.' Isis leaned forward and reached for the waistband. Most of it was strung with cowrie shells, but there was a little amulet right in the middle. 'It *is* mine, look. I know it is, because Hopi gave me that scarab.' She fingered the amulet, turning it over so that the scarab shape could be seen clearly.

Mut pulled a face. 'My waistbands have scarabs on them, too.'

'But not *this* scarab,' insisted Isis, feeling annoyed. She knew exactly why Mut was being difficult – it was because she'd mentioned Hopi. It happened every single time. 'This one belonged to my father. Look, it's got a little hieroglyph on the side.'

Mut stared at it, then frowned and snatched the waistband away.

Isis tried to grab it back, but Mut wouldn't let go.

'Careful!' cried Isis.

Too late. The band was still tangled up with the collar, and it caught on the collar's fine threads. One of the threads broke. Blue and red beads scattered everywhere, all across the floor. The two girls gazed at them in horror.

Mut was the first to speak. 'Now look what you've done!'

'What *I've* done?' Isis was furious. 'You did it as much as me – you snatched –'

'It was your fault for grabbing! I'll tell Mother.'

'It was both of us,' said Isis. 'You know it was. Don't you *dare* tell Nefert I did it.'

Mut smirked. 'And what if I do?' she asked coolly.

Isis was enraged. 'I'll tell Hopi to put a snake in your bed!'

As soon as the words were out of her mouth, she regretted them. Mut's face tightened with fear. Recently, Hopi had brought a snake home, and shown it to Mut. She had almost screamed the house down. He had said it wouldn't hurt her, but Mut was inconsolable, and didn't want anything to do with Hopi any more. She said he was creepy.

It made life very difficult for Isis. She loved her brother Hopi more than anyone else in the world, and she was used to his love of lizards and snakes and scorpions. Other people didn't seem to feel the same way, and she often had to spring to his defence. Mut was particularly hard work. Whenever Hopi came into the conversation, they almost always started arguing.

Still, it was much better than the life she'd had before. Two seasons ago, when the River Nile was just starting its annual flood, Isis had been spotted on the street by Paneb, the head of a dance and music troupe. He was looking for a dance partner for his daughter Mut, and Isis was perfect; the two girls were both eleven years old, small, supple and slender. But she wouldn't go anywhere without Hopi, so Paneb had taken them both into the family. It had seemed like a miracle. After the death of their parents, Hopi and Isis had been forced to live with an old, poverty-stricken uncle out on the fringes of Waset. Too sick to work, he had relied on his niece and nephew to beg for an income. The uncle had since died, and his mud-brick house was slowly returning to the earth from which it was made.

So Isis just had to live with the squabbles. Mut turned away, and began to pick up the beads from her mother's broken collar. Isis bent down to help her, her thoughts seething.

Hopi slowed down as he left the town behind him. The great River Nile glinted in the sunlight to his right, while fields of flax and wheat waved gently in the breeze to his left. He sat down by an irrigation ditch, opened his bag and lifted the lid off the basket.

'There'll be plenty to eat out here,' he told the snake. 'Lots of mice and frogs and maybe some rats, if you're lucky.'

This time, he didn't use his stick, but reached for the snake with his bare hands. It was perfectly true that it was harmless. It curled itself around his fingers, then, as he placed it near the ground, it slithered off between the lush plants that grew along the ditch.

Hopi watched it go, rubbing his injured leg where it ached from walking. It made him think about the day when the crocodile god Sobek had taken his parents to the next world. They were now *hesyu*, or blessed drowned ones. A crocodile had seized Hopi, too, but the effect it had had was strange. It was as though Sobek had touched him in some special way, and he had developed an affinity with all feared creatures. His favourites were snakes and scorpions. He spent his time hunting them out and learning their ways; he knew their habits and what they ate, he knew which ones could kill and which could not.

It was frustrating when people didn't trust his knowledge. Of course they were scared, but why couldn't they see simple differences? Not every snake was a cobra. Many snakes did more good than harm, eating the vermin that lived around people's houses. Of course, they might believe him if he were an adult, but he was just a poor boy with a limp. The only person who understood was Isis.

He fished around in his bag for the woman's amulet. It was a roughly glazed piece of faience with the shape of a scorpion moulded on to the top. Hopi examined it carefully, disappointment welling up inside. The amulet was scuffed and chipped. It wasn't even something he could sell in the market in exchange for a few pieces of fruit. He'd have to return home empty-handed, as he did nearly every day, with nothing to contribute to the family income. He was just a burden, dependent on the work of his little sister.

Isis and Mut were still picking up blue and red beads when Mut's mother Nefert walked in. They looked up guiltily.

'My best collar!' she exclaimed. 'What happened?'

The two girls spoke at once.

'Isis did it.'

'It was an accident!'

Isis glared at Mut, whose eyes flashed in defiance.

Nefert folded her arms. 'What happened?' she repeated.

'It was both of us,' said Isis. 'It was tangled in my old waistband –'

'*My* waistband!' cried Mut.

'Mine,' said Isis, raising her voice, 'and it wasn't just my fault, Mut grabbed it back –'

'That's not true, you snatched it!' shouted Mut.

'STOP it, both of you!' Nefert's voice silenced them.

Isis felt her heart beating hard inside her chest, her anger fighting to get out. Mut couldn't get away with this, she just couldn't. It was too unfair.

Nefert's mouth was tight with annoyance. She looked from one girl to the other and back again, letting them see just how cross she was. Isis waited, dread slowly replacing her anger. She began to wonder what the punishment would be.

Then Mut spoke, her voice soft and pitiful. 'Isis said that if I told you, she'd get Hopi to put a snake in my bed.'

The words hung in the air. Isis went cold inside. How could Mut tell on her like that! She felt like grabbing her hair and yanking it hard.

'Isis, is that true?'

'I didn't mean it. Anyway, it wasn't just me, it was both of us. Mut knows it was but she was angry because Hopi gave me that scarab –' The words tumbled out.

'Now look.' Nefert's voice was shaking with anger.

'I'm deeply disappointed in both of you. That was my best collar. But you, Isis . . .' She shook her head. 'I can't believe you would say something so nasty. You know that Mut is terrified of snakes.'

Isis hung her head. 'Sorry, Nefert. I really didn't mean it.'

'If we didn't have a party tomorrow night, you wouldn't be eating for the rest of the day. As it is, I want you to understand that I won't have that sort of behaviour in this house. And don't you ever, *ever* threaten Mut with snakes again. Do you hear me?'

Isis nodded, relieved that this time she was going to get away with it. 'Yes, Nefert.'

'Now, I want you to finish sorting out the box. Collect all the beads from my collar. I'll have to get it rethreaded. Then go and help Sheri prepare lunch. We've all got a lot to do. I want you to rehearse your new routine once more this evening. We're setting out for Set Maat at daybreak tomorrow.'

Hopi stepped out of the sun and into the shadow of the house. He moved quietly, as he always did; he might not be able to move fast, but years of tracking desert creatures had taught him to move stealthily. He listened to the noises of the household, trying to work out where everyone was. Nefert's widowed sisters,

Sheri and Kia, were scouring pots in the courtyard, talking and laughing together. He couldn't hear Isis nor Mut, nor Mut's two young brothers. Perhaps they were asleep.

'. . . my best collar,' drifted a voice from the room at the front of the house. That was Nefert.

One of the cats padded up and rubbed against Hopi's leg. He bent down to tickle it behind the ears.

'Rethreading it is not so difficult,' murmured the voice of Paneb, Nefert's husband. 'Can't you . . .'

Hopi missed the end of the sentence. He stroked the cat to the tip of its tail and straightened up. He was hungry. He had meant to come home for the midday meal, but he'd ended up rescuing the snake from that woman's house instead. He hoped that there would still be some food around, if he asked Sheri nicely.

Nefert's voice broke into his thoughts again. 'No, of course not. I've already sent the girls to get it fixed,' she said. 'But to be honest I'm more bothered about Isis.' Her voice sounded serious, and Hopi went stiff. What had his sister been up to?

'I don't know how long it can go on like this,' Nefert's voice continued. 'Ever since Hopi brought that snake in, they've been arguing. I thought Isis would be a good friend to Mut, but it's not working out that way.'

'Girls of the same age always squabble,' said Paneb.

'Not like this. I don't like it, Paneb. Isis is so loyal to Hopi, and Mut doesn't get on with either of them. She's on her own, and I think it's making her unhappy. And as for Hopi and his snakes . . .'

'Well, what are you thinking of doing about it?' asked Paneb. 'Isis has learnt the routines well. It would be difficult to replace her, surely?'

Hopi suddenly felt sick. *Replace Isis?* But this was their only home! He craned his neck to hear Nefert's reply, but her voice had faded to a mumble.

'Don't do anything rash, Nefert,' came Paneb's voice. 'Think about it.'

Hopi swallowed hard. He couldn't bear to hear any more. Quickly, he walked through the house and out to the courtyard. He raised a hand in greeting to Sheri and Kia, then climbed up the stairway that led to the upper storey and the roof. His appetite had gone.

'And again! Together this time!' Nefert's voice rang out.

Isis and Mut spun around, their arms in the air, then both somersaulted forward in perfect hand-springs. No sooner had they landed than they arched themselves backwards and flipped the other way. They landed on their feet, then swung their hips and raised their arms again in time to imaginary music. Nefert clapped to get them to stop.

'Much better,' she said. 'There won't be much room to dance at these parties, from what I've heard. The houses of Set Maat are small, so you must keep close together and keep your movements tight.'

The girls nodded.

'And I want you to be on your best behaviour. You will be guests for three nights in the village and you must make a good impression. They are paying us well. We want to make sure they invite us back. Do you understand?'

Isis and Mut nodded again.

'No arguing. No fighting. I haven't forgotten what happened this afternoon.'

Isis lowered her gaze. She was still annoyed with Mut, but she knew she mustn't show it.

'You can go now,' said Nefert. 'I want you to go to sleep early. Tomorrow will be a very long day.'

Isis turned and skipped out of the room. She climbed up on to the roof and found her brother leaning over the low wall at its edge, watching the street below. Dusk had fallen, and twinkling lamps were shining like little stars along the winding streets. She ran up to Hopi lightly and clapped her hands around his head, hiding his eyes.

'Isis! Let go,' he protested, tugging at her arms.

'How d'you know it's me?' teased Isis.

Hopi pulled her arms free and turned round to face her. 'Don't joke, Isis,' he said in a quiet voice. He looked across the roof to check that they were alone. 'I need to talk to you.'

Isis saw that he meant it. 'What's wrong?' she demanded.

'That's what I want *you* to tell *me*,' said Hopi. 'What happened with Mut today?'

Isis pulled a face. She'd had enough of thinking about Mut. 'Oh, it was stupid,' she said. 'We had a fight and broke one of Nefert's collars. She sent us to get it mended. Everything's fine now.'

Hopi shook his head. 'No, Isis, it isn't fine.'

'Why? What do you know about it?'

'I heard Nefert talking to Paneb. She thinks you and Mut argue too much . . .'

All at once, Isis was furious again. 'But it's not my fault! It's always Mut who starts it! She's just jealous.'

Hopi snorted. 'There's nothing for Mut to be jealous of, Isis.'

'Yes, there is. She's jealous of you. Jealous of us, I mean. She doesn't have a brother or sister she's close to. Ramose and Kha are too young.'

'It's more than that, Isis. She's afraid of me. You know she is. And Nefert's beginning to worry.'

Isis examined Hopi's face, and saw how unhappy he looked. Suddenly, she felt full of fear. She put her arms around her brother and laid her head against his chest.

'What did Paneb say?' she whispered.

Hopi was silent for a few seconds. 'He tried to defend us a little,' he murmured eventually, his voice hoarse. 'But we need to be careful, Isis. We depend on this house.'

Isis heard her brother's heart thumping in his chest, and clung on tighter.

'I'm sorry.' Hopi's voice was full of sorrow and shame. 'But I can't bear to go back to begging. And I don't know how else I'd support you if they replaced you with someone else.'

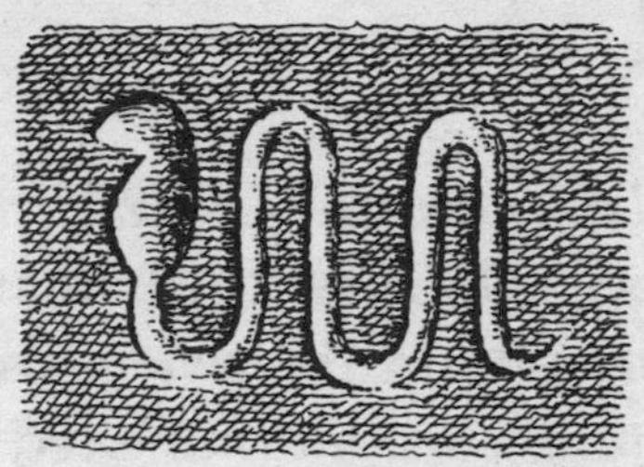

CHAPTER TWO

Isis closed her eyes, trying to fight back the panic. When she opened them, the River Nile still stretched out in front of her, calm and wide, with the palm trees and fields of the west bank on the other side; the desert hills beyond glowed orange-pink in the light of the early morning sun. She saw this view every day – but it was one thing looking at the Nile, and quite another getting into a boat to cross it. She tried to breathe slowly, in . . . out, in . . . out . . .

'I'm here, Isis,' said Hopi. 'It's going to be fine. The crocodiles live further upstream. Nothing's going to happen to you.'

Isis gripped his arm. She knew her brother was speaking, but his words didn't sink in. All she could see was swirling water, and all she could hear was her

father's voice: *Look after Isis! Look after Isis . . .*

Those had been the last words that he had cried amid the catastrophe in the river. Isis would never forget the churning waters turning red as her parents were pulled underwater, nor the snapping teeth of the crocodile that had seized her brother, but then, miraculously, let go.

Hopi was shaking her. 'Isis. Come on. We have to do this. Everyone's waiting for us.'

Isis looked at him, gulping air. 'I can't.'

'You can. You *must*.' He lowered his voice. 'Isis, remember what I told you last night. I'm counting on you.'

Another, different fear pulled Isis out of her terror. She looked down from the riverbank at the barge that served as the ferry. There were Paneb and Nefert, waiting patiently. There were their two young sons, Ramose and Kha, sitting astride the hired donkey. Sheri was smiling, as always, and waving encouragement, while Kia sat gazing over the water . . . and Mut . . . Mut was leaning over the prow of the boat, watching Isis with a grin on her face.

That did it. Isis pursed her lips. How could Mut mock her like that, when *she* was frightened of snakes! Hopi was right. She *must* get on that boat, even if it killed her – which was exactly what she feared it might do. Holding Hopi's hand tightly, she stepped forward, down the bank. As she clambered on board, the ferryman steadied the barge for her, but it still wobbled horribly. Isis let out a little scream.

Paneb took her arm and held her firmly. 'You're safe, Isis. We're all safe.'

Isis plucked up all her courage and stepped further along the barge.

'Well done,' murmured Hopi.

Sheri reached for Isis and gave her a hug. 'Come and sit next to me,' she said. 'We'll be over the river in no time. Here, have some dates.'

Isis smiled faintly, but shook her head. She felt sick. She sat down next to Sheri and buried her head in her hands as the boat began to move.

Hopi sat down on the other side of his sister, one arm around her shoulders. He was trying hard to behave normally, but his insides were in a tight knot. It wasn't his sister's fear that made him feel this way. Since overhearing Nefert, he had felt as though his world were coming apart. He and Isis trusted this family as though it were their own; in the space of a few months, Paneb and Nefert had come to seem like parents, and Sheri and Kia like aunts – especially Sheri, who was always so warm and loving. But

Nefert's words had shown Hopi the truth. They only belonged because of Isis and the work she did with Mut. If that fell apart, so would everything else.

The little wooden barge glided across the smooth, deep waters, and the west bank drew closer. The west, where the sun set, was the Kingdom of the Dead, and the rose-pink mountains were the final resting place of Egypt's great kings. The tomb-builders lived in the very village they were heading to now: Set Maat, the Place of Truth.

The craftsmen led a charmed, well-paid life away from everyone else, and Hopi felt a pang of envy. If only he had a craft that he could use to support Isis! Their father had been a wig-maker, but he hadn't passed on his skills before he died. He'd had other ambitions for his son. 'Wig-making is a dead-end job,' he had always said to Hopi. 'I want you to be a scribe.'

And so he had worked hard to pay for his son to study. Hopi had completed two years; he had learned many of the basic hieroglyphs, and had mastered the inks and reed pen. But with the death of his parents, his studies had stopped. Five years had clouded his memory; he could barely read now. And with his injured leg, he was of no use to most other trades. He wasn't strong enough for any kind of manual work.

'Are we nearly there?' whispered Isis.

Hopi gripped her shoulders. 'Yes. Only a few more minutes.'

He stood up as the barge approached the river-bank. *I will find something to do,* he swore to himself. *I must find something to do. Whatever happens, I must look after Isis.*

As soon as she was on the riverbank, Isis felt a rush of relief. 'I did it! I did it!' she cried. She hugged Hopi and Sheri, then skipped up to Happy, the hired donkey, and begged Paneb to let her lead him.

Paneb smiled at her kindly, and handed her the lead rope. 'You were very brave, Isis,' he said. 'We're all proud of you.'

Isis took the rope, smiling back. Paneb might not love her quite as much as he loved his own daughter, but he was very fair. She tugged on Happy's rope and started walking. She didn't want to think too hard about Nefert.

'Make him go fast!' called Ramose, the five-year-old.

Little Kha giggled. 'Yes! Fast!' he chirruped, bouncing up and down on Happy's back.

Isis grinned. The donkey was old, and stubborn. 'Happy won't go fast for anyone,' she said. 'Not even you.'

The troupe trudged towards Set Maat through fields of emmer wheat and past shimmering mortuary temples. At last they reached the desert, where nothing but yellow-white dust and pebbles crunched under their sandals. A well-used road wound up towards the limestone cliffs. It was as though the village were in the heart of the mountain itself. Isis shivered with excitement. This place seemed full of magic.

A workman came to greet them and led the way to the gate, where Medjay policemen were posted as guards. They looked over each member of the family and checked the bags on Happy's back before allowing them through. Isis was impressed. This village took itself very seriously. They walked through the gate and along a narrow street lined with small white-washed houses.

'You will stay in three different houses,' explained the workman. He nodded at Isis, Hopi and Mut. 'The three young people will stay here.' And he knocked on a red wooden door.

Isis felt her heart sink. The man couldn't have picked a worse combination. Why couldn't Mut stay with her aunts instead? Now there was bound to be trouble. She sneaked a glance at Mut, and saw that she was looking miserable, too. But neither of them had any choice in the matter.

A girl peered out of the red door. She was pretty, slightly plump and her skin had the sheen of someone who used expensive oils on it every day. She greeted the crowd with a big smile, and Isis liked her at once.

'Are these our guests?' the girl asked. 'How exciting! I'm Heria. Come in!'

Isis, Hopi and Mut followed Heria into the little house. Isis gazed around in amazement. The house might be small, but the walls were painted with exquisite murals, and the furniture was all of the highest quality. Of course. It made sense. The village was home to some of the best craftsmen in the whole of Egypt, so their houses were bound to be special.

Heria led them to a small back room lined with reed mats and low, simple beds. 'We're all going to sleep in here,' she said. She looked at the three of them in turn. 'You're so alike. You must be sisters,' she said, looking from Isis to Mut.

'We're not,' said Mut at once. 'We're only dance partners. I'm Mut.' And she gave Heria a dazzling smile.

Mut looked lovely when she smiled. Heria smiled back, enchanted, and all at once Isis saw an answer to her problem – at least for the next few days. Mut and

Heria could become friends! Then Mut would be happier and, for once, Isis and Hopi could spend time together in peace.

Hopi was at a loose end. Mut and Isis had gone to see where they would be performing that evening, and Heria was preparing food for her father's return from the kings' tombs. He wandered out on to the main street and looked around. The village nestled between a hill on one side and the mountain on the other, its lower slopes dotted with little chapels and the dark entrances to the villagers' tombs.

Hopi walked up the street, looking for some way up on to the mountain. Women stared at him from their doorways, and young children ran behind him, calling out. Hopi was used to being followed, so he spun round and pulled a face, waving his arms. The children ran away at once, shrieking and laughing in terror.

Beyond the cemetery, Hopi could just see a track leading up on to the cliffs. The limestone rocks were perfect hiding places for lizards and scorpions – and snakes, of course. It would be good to spend a few hours up there. He found a side street that led him to an unguarded gateway and climbed up slowly, nursing his leg, which was sore after the morning's long walk.

Chapter Two

In the heat of the afternoon, the chapel courtyards were deserted. Voices from the village drifted up, but around the tombs Hopi was aware of a strange stillness. He wiped the sweat from his forehead, trying to ignore the feeling that was creeping over him. He couldn't say why, but he was sure he was being watched.

He began to walk faster and suddenly came across the cliff path winding its way up the mountainside. Slowly, carefully, he followed it.

He didn't get far.

'Hey!' called a voice, somewhere nearby.

Hopi spun round, his heart thumping. There was no one there. He stood still for a moment, surveying the view below. Still nothing. Nervously, he began climbing again.

'Where are you going?' The voice was loud and clear this time.

Hopi stopped. 'Where are you?' he called.

For a few seconds, nothing happened. Then, from behind some rugged boulders, a young man stepped out.

'Who gave you permission to climb this pathway?' he asked gruffly.

Hopi shook his head. 'No one.'

The young man stared at him. 'So how did you get past the Medjay guards?'

'There weren't any,' said Hopi. 'I came through that gateway there.' And he pointed down at the cemetery gate.

'You were in the village already?'

'Yes. I've come with the music and dance troupe from Waset.'

'Ah, I see!' The young man's expression cleared. 'Well, I'm surprised no one warned you. You're not supposed to wander around up here – it's out of bounds to strangers. This path leads to the Great Place, where the kings are buried.'

'I'm sorry. I'll go back down, I was only looking for snakes and scorpions . . .'

The young man examined Hopi more closely. 'Really? What do you know about snakes and scorpions?'

Hopi shrugged. 'Well, quite a lot, I suppose.'

'You've been trained?'

'No, no – I've just taught myself.'

The man stroked his chin, looking thoughtful. Then a mysterious glint appeared in his eye. 'Strange,' he muttered. 'This could be . . .'

'Could be what?' Hopi was curious.

The man shook his head. 'Oh, nothing. Let me introduce myself. My name's Seti. I'm a painter up at the tombs – I've just finished my apprenticeship. I'll show you a bit more of the mountain, if you like.'

Hopi nodded. 'I'm Hopi. Thank you. I'd like that.'

Seti smiled, then turned and began to climb energetically. Hopi struggled to keep up, cursing his injury. Seti looked back and waited for him. 'Sorry,' he said, nodding at Hopi's leg, then continued more slowly, taking a side path that led around to the left, out of sight of the village. Perching himself on a ledge, Seti patted the space next to him. Hopi sat down, and rested his elbows on his knees to get his breath back.

Seti was quiet for a few moments. Then he spoke, just one word. 'Meretseger,' he said.

The word meant *she who loves silence*.

Hopi frowned. 'Who's she?'

'You don't know of her?'

Hopi shook his head.

Seti gestured up at the mountainside behind them. 'This is her home,' he said. 'She is the cobra goddess of the mountain. She has many names, but Meretseger is the most powerful. Sometimes we call her after her home: the Peak of the West.'

Hopi was astonished. The only cobra goddess he had ever heard of was Renenutet, the goddess of the harvest. 'We don't worship her in Waset,' he said.

'No. There's no reason why you should. But if you

know so much about snakes, perhaps you could help me meet her.'

'You wish to hunt out cobras? But why?' Hopi was puzzled. 'Doesn't Meretseger have a shrine or temple where you can worship her?'

'Yes, yes. It's over there.' Seti nodded towards the south. 'I make offerings there every week. But that's not enough.' He studied his hands, and seemed to be trying to decide what to say. 'I need to see her for myself. I need to know . . . I am seeking an answer . . .'

Hopi was intrigued. 'An answer to what?'

Seti hesitated. He looked out over the view, a frown on his face. Then he turned to Hopi and spoke in a low, confidential tone. 'You are younger than I,' he said. 'But I see from your leg that life's troubles have already touched you.'

'Indeed they have,' agreed Hopi, with feeling.

'And perhaps some of the gods seem more important than others,' suggested Seti. 'Some bring blessings, while others bring pain.'

Hopi nodded. 'The god Sobek has brought me both,' he said, for the crocodile god had taken much away from him, but had also given him his unusual gift.

'Then you understand,' said Seti, relief in his voice. 'Now, if I tell you that a crisis has brought me to seek out Meretseger, you will accept what I say.'

Hopi thought about it. He had great respect for all the gods, and Seti's words were still a little confusing. 'The cobra is a powerful snake. This must be a powerful goddess. I would not want to attract her attention without good reason.'

His words seemed to trouble Seti. 'No, no, you wouldn't,' he agreed, fear clouding his face. 'She's terrible when she's angry. And . . . and that's what I need to know – if she is truly angry.'

'If she is angry? With who? You?'

Seti looked uneasy. 'I can't tell you that,' he said. He sighed, a little wearily, and stood up. 'All I can say is that I feel that she has sent you. So will you help me, or not?'

Mut was helping Heria with her make-up, patting red ochre powder on to her cheeks.

'Not too much!' exclaimed Heria. She grabbed her polished bronze mirror and peered at her reflection. Mut had already finished her eyes, which were surrounded with dramatic black eyeliner and a touch of green malachite paint.

'You look beautiful,' declared Mut. 'Doesn't she, Isis?'

Isis nodded and smiled. 'Lovely,' she agreed. She

was watching Mut in surprise. She couldn't remember the last time her dance partner had seemed so happy. Mut was fussing around Heria, dabbing at her cheeks and then her lips with the red ochre, her face alight with friendliness.

'I wish I had a sister,' said Heria wistfully. 'You two must do each other's make-up all the time.'

Mut's smile disappeared. 'I told you,' she said sharply. 'We're not sisters. We're just dance partners.'

A flicker of surprise crossed Heria's face. 'Yes, but . . . you live together, don't you?'

Mut pursed her lips. 'We haven't for long. And anyway, Isis has Hopi,' she said.

'Mut!' Isis couldn't keep quiet any longer. 'What's Hopi got to do with it? He doesn't do my make-up, does he?'

'So *do* you do it for each other?' Heria looked at Isis, clearly puzzled.

'Of course we do,' said Isis.

Mut went very quiet. All her good humour had vanished, and there was an awkward silence. Then Mut reached for the wig that lay by Heria's side. 'It's time to put your wig on,' she said.

Quietly, Isis slipped out of the room. *Leave them to it*, she thought, and went out to the courtyard to find a beaker of water. As she did so, there was a soft knock on the front door. She went to open it, and found a boy of about Hopi's age.

He grinned at her. 'Is Mut there?' he asked. 'Nefert's sent me.'

'Yes,' said Isis, letting him in. 'She's in the back room with Heria.'

The boy obviously knew where he was going. Isis trailed after him as he walked straight through the house.

'Hello, Heria,' he greeted her. 'Nefert's sent me to get Mut. She wants her to help her get ready for the party.'

Heria smiled at Mut. 'Looks like you've finished just in time,' she said.

Mut looked disappointed, and Isis could guess why. Helping Nefert meant leaving her new-found friend – and more than that, it meant leaving her alone with Isis. Mut fiddled with the beads on Heria's wig for a moment, her face averted. Then she followed the boy out without a word.

When the front door had closed, Heria turned to Isis, playing with the ends of her wig. 'Is Mut always like that?' she asked bluntly.

'Like what?'

Heria hesitated. 'Well . . . she wasn't very nice to you.'

Isis felt embarrassed. 'Oh, Mut's just in a bad mood,' she said. 'We had an argument yesterday.'

'That's a shame,' said Heria. She looked sad. 'I'd love to live with someone my own age. I've got friends, of course, but it's not the same.'

Isis was suddenly aware of how quiet the little house was. It was unusual for an Egyptian household. Isis thought of their street in Waset, and how all the houses buzzed with people. But here, there was no one around apart from Heria's father Khonsu, who had come back from the tombs and fallen asleep in the front room.

'Who *does* live here?' she asked. 'Just the two of you?'

Heria nodded. She stood up and straightened the beautiful black wig. Some of the hairs at the back were tangled, and Isis went to tease them out for her.

'And Father's so busy at the moment. He's up at the tombs most of the time, but even when he's here, he's stuck in secret meetings in the front room.'

'Secret meetings? That sounds exciting,' said Isis.

'Huh. Not really. He doesn't tell me what they're about.' Then Heria lowered her voice. 'Though sometimes I overhear things.'

'What kind of things?'

'Well . . .' Heria hesitated. 'Didn't you think it was

odd that you and your family were invited here?'

Isis frowned and shook her head. The dance troupe got invitations to all sorts of places; this one didn't seem any different. 'Why? Don't you invite people usually?'

'No. We have our own musicians.'

'So what's happened to them?'

Heria sighed. 'Well . . . one of the families is sick. And one of the other dancers, Tiya, has broken her arm.' Suddenly, her voice wobbled. 'Tiya's my best friend. Her arm might never be the same again, and no one will want to watch a dancer with a crooked arm.'

Straight away, Isis thought of Hopi's injured leg, and her heart flooded with sympathy. She put a hand on Heria's shoulder.

'That's not even the worst of it,' Heria carried on. 'I know that Father's having people watched. It's awful. I know lots of families are being spied on, and I can't say a word.'

'Spied on!' exclaimed Isis. 'But why?'

'I wish I knew,' said Heria. She wiped away a tear that had trickled down her cheek. 'Now I've smudged my make-up, haven't I?'

Isis smiled. 'I'll soon fix it for you.' She bent down and picked up a piece of soft linen that Heria kept with her make-up pots. She moistened it, then began dabbing around Heria's eyes.

'You and Mut are both so lovely,' said Heria gratefully. 'I'm glad you're here.'

Isis felt awkward and ashamed. 'I'm always fighting with Mut,' she confessed. 'She doesn't like Hopi, that's the trouble. But I have to be nice to her now, whatever she says. Hopi thinks that if I'm not careful, we'll get thrown out of the troupe.'

Heria's eyes widened in shock. 'But . . . they're your family!' she exclaimed.

'Not really.' Isis explained about her parents, her uncle and how she had been taken in as a dance partner for Mut. 'We haven't lived with them for long,' she said. 'And Hopi can't work, so they just keep him for my sake. Now Nefert's getting angry because Mut and I don't get on.'

'But where would you go?'

It was a question that Isis had been avoiding. She hadn't wanted to face up to Hopi's warning. It hadn't seemed real, until now.

'I think we might have relatives, somewhere,' she said, uncertainly. 'But not in Waset.'

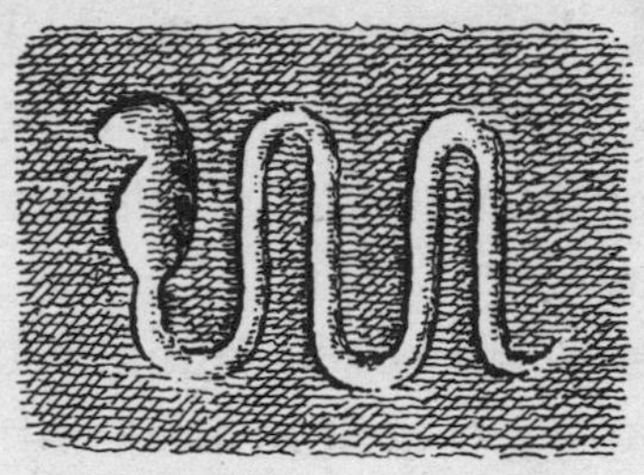

CHAPTER THREE

The house of Nakht was packed, and the inner room was hot. Very hot. Lamplight flickered around the walls, creating deep, twisting shadows that leaped and cavorted in time with the music. Nefert, Sheri and Kia were playing their instruments faster and faster, while Paneb beat out the rhythm with a pair of clappers. Mut and Isis gyrated and swayed to the music, their bodies shining with fragrant oil.

The room was crowded with people. Men holding beakers of wine stood cheering and clapping. Women sat along one wall dressed in their finest linen and jewellery – beautiful beaded collars and gold bangles that glinted in the lamplight. Perfume cones sat on top of their wigs, slowly melting, filling the room with rich, sweet scent.

'More space! More space!' Paneb cried. 'Make room for our dancers!'

The partygoers squeezed tighter together, laughing, to create an open area in the centre of the room. Mut and Isis whirled into it together, perfectly in time. They gave each other a little nod and flipped their bodies forward into a front-flip. Then, without pausing, they flipped themselves backwards in the tiny space, gaining a roar of applause.

'Again!' called the men.

The girls did as the men asked, then carried on with their dance. Their arms in the air, they swung their hips in time to the music, then started taking rhythmic little steps, first in one direction, then in the other. Isis knew this part of their routine so well that she could allow her glance to wander around the room. Some of the women had drunk too much wine, and were giggling together in a corner. Many of the men had started leaning against the walls a little heavily. By the doorway stood Hopi, alone.

In between her twists and turns, Isis noticed someone appear by Hopi's side: a middle-aged man, wearing a neat, well-made wig and fine jewellery. Hopi looked surprised as the man started talking to him. Isis saw him shaking his head, his face concerned. What was going on?

She had to carry on dancing. They were reaching a more difficult section of their routine, and she needed to concentrate. But now the man was placing a heavy hand on Hopi's shoulder . . .

Isis wished they could dance in that direction. She craned her neck, distracted. Before she knew it, she was out of time. She did a somersault well after Mut, and landed awkwardly, almost falling over. Mut glared at her, furious. She could tell what her dance partner meant: *What do you think you're doing?*

Isis felt her cheeks grow hot, hoping desperately that Nefert and Paneb hadn't noticed. Arguing with Mut was one thing. Making mistakes when she was dancing was quite another. The troupe prided itself on giving a perfect performance every time – its reputation depended upon it. Losing concentration like that . . . Isis was furious with herself. It was unforgivable.

'Come with me.'

The man steered Hopi out of the main room. Hopi looked over his shoulder, hoping to see someone familiar, but the whole family was performing, and he hadn't seen Seti since they'd parted that afternoon. The man dug his fingers a little deeper into Hopi's shoulder. There was no choice. This man had an air of authority, something powerful that was slightly frightening. Obediently, Hopi accompanied him out into the cool night air.

In the moonlight, the man's eyes searched Hopi's face from beneath dark eyebrows. 'It worries me when I see young people dabbling in things that they do not understand,' he said.

Hopi was baffled. 'Are you speaking to the right person, sir?' he asked. 'I only arrived this morning. I'm not dabbling in anything.'

'Oh, I'm addressing the right person, there's no doubt about that.'

Hopi began to feel very uncomfortable. The man's eyes seemed to be boring straight through him.

'Well . . . the only thing I've done is look for snakes,' he said. 'I know I shouldn't have been on the cliff path, but I meant no harm.'

'I know what you were doing,' said the man. 'What's unfortunate is that you yourself do not. There is powerful magic at work in this village, boy.'

Hopi was beginning to feel scared. 'What kind of magic, sir?' he asked.

The man placed a hand on his shoulder once more. 'You do not belong here,' he said. 'The secrets of this village have nothing to do with you. Try to remember that.'

'Yes, but –'

'Don't ask questions. Do not follow strangers who may lead you into trouble. And, above all, fear and respect the magic that surrounds us here. You are not in Waset now, but treading in the Kingdom of the Dead, where the greatest of our kings find access to the Next World. This mountain . . .' he said, waving a hand towards the dark rocky bulk behind them, 'is a sacred place.'

Hopi realised that his mouth had gone dry. The only stranger he had followed was Seti, who was not much older than himself. How could that get him into trouble? It wasn't even as though they'd found any snakes – they'd hunted all afternoon without any luck. He licked his lips, and found nothing to say.

The man directed him back into the party. 'I see you've understood me well enough. Now go and enjoy yourself. Drink wine, and watch your sister perform.'

The mention of Isis gave Hopi a little courage. 'Who are you?' he managed to ask.

'I am Rahotep,' the man answered. 'I hope you will remember my name.'

Hopi nodded. 'I will, sir.'

'Good. Now go.'

Hopi was only too glad to obey. He stepped back

towards the house of Nakht, but in the darkness a rut in the street made him stumble. His weak leg collapsed beneath him and, with a cry, he fell to the ground.

For a second, he was winded. Then he felt Rahotep's hand on his arm. 'Are you hurt?' asked the man.

Hopi sat up slowly, brushing himself down. He winced as he moved his bad leg, but could tell that he had not done any real harm.

'No . . . no. I'm all right.' He reached for his linen bag, which had flown off his shoulder. Some of its contents had spilled on the ground, and Rahotep helped him gather them up: some pottery ostraca on which Hopi sometimes doodled, and the lid of his papyrus basket. He took them and put them back into his bag, then spotted the cheap amulet that the woman had given him the day before. He bent down to pick it up, and Rahotep saw it.

'What is that?' he demanded.

Hopi shrugged. 'Nothing. Just an amulet. A woman gave it to me yesterday. It's worthless.'

'Let me see it.' Rahotep held out his hand.

Puzzled, Hopi passed it over. The man looked at it closely. When he looked up, something in his expression had changed. Now, he looked almost . . . *curious*.

'Why did she give it to you?' he asked.

Hopi shrugged. 'It was all she could find. She didn't want to give me anything at all, if you ask me.'

Rahotep shook his head. 'You have not understood,' he said. 'I asked why she gave you *that*. It was not a random gift. What was it for?'

'Oh, I see.' Hopi nodded. 'You're right, it was more of a payment than a gift. She had a snake in her house and I took it away for her. It was a perfectly harmless rat-eating snake, that's all.'

Rahotep nodded, slowly. He handed the amulet back. Once more, he placed his hand on Hopi's shoulder, but this time it felt more gentle.

'You asked who I am,' he said, and now his voice was gentler, too.

'Yes. You are Rahotep,' said Hopi.

'True. I am Rahotep, a workman in the Great Place. But I am also a priest of the goddess Serqet. Do you know what this means?'

Hopi cursed his ignorance. It frustrated him that he knew so little, and he mourned his lost education. So Serqet was a goddess, but, like Meretseger, he had never heard the name before.

'No, sir.'

'I thought as much.' Rahotep helped him to his

feet. 'Well, the gods reveal themselves in their own time.' And he turned to lead Hopi back into the light and noise of the party.

The routine was coming to an end. Isis and Mut held hands to smile and bow; the foreman Nakht himself stepped forward to place flower garlands around their necks. Isis glanced at Nefert to see if she seemed annoyed, but both she and Paneb were smiling at their host. Perhaps they hadn't seen her slip, after all.

The partygoers began to mill around, finding new people to talk to. Isis looked for Hopi, but he was nowhere in sight. Servants appeared carrying trays of delicious-smelling food and flagons of wine; a young girl offered Mut and Isis some freshly cut melon.

Mut took a slice, and sucked on it thirstily. 'You made a mistake,' she said.

There was no point in denying it. It would only make things worse. 'I know,' Isis admitted, her cheeks flaring up in shame. 'I'm sorry, Mut.'

Mut looked surprised at the apology. 'So what happened?'

'I got distracted. I saw . . .' Isis bit back her words in time. She couldn't possibly admit the mistake was because of Hopi. Quickly, she made something up. 'I . . . I saw someone drop their wine.'

'What kind of excuse is that?' demanded Mut in disgust. 'It looked really bad, Isis. We can't afford to make mistakes. Our jobs depend on it.'

Isis knew that, for once, Mut was right. She almost felt like crying. But at the same time, part of her felt that Mut *wanted* Isis to get into trouble. Maybe she wanted to get rid of her altogether.

'I suppose you're going to run straight to Nefert and Paneb,' she said, her voice trembling. 'You're going to tell, aren't you?'

'Tell what?' asked a cheerful voice.

Mut's face lit up. 'Heria!' she exclaimed.

'Well, come on, tell me,' Heria probed, smiling from one girl to the other.

It was easy to read Mut's mind. Her face was a picture of indecision. Half of her wanted to gloat, but the other half wanted Heria to think well of her. Isis couldn't bear the tension.

'I made a mistake when we were dancing,' she blurted out. 'Did you see it?'

'Oh no! You looked wonderful to me,' said Heria. She put a friendly arm around Mut's shoulder. 'Why, it's not serious, is it?'

Mut looked caught out. 'Well . . . it depends who saw it,' she said lamely.

Heria laughed. 'Don't worry about that! Most of

the guests can hardly see straight,' she pointed out. 'Nakht has been serving his best wine. Everyone thinks you're both lovely. And very talented, too.'

'Oh.' Mut looked pleased, and Isis shot Heria a grateful glance. Heria winked back at her, and Isis saw that she had understood the situation perfectly. What a relief. It was good to know she had an ally.

Heria linked arms with both of them. 'Come, I want you to meet my friend,' she said, and led them out of the room.

Out in the courtyard, some of the servants were roasting fowl and mutton, while others prepared vegetables. The space was tiny, but somehow the servants managed to keep trays of food circulating among the guests. Heria dived around them, and Isis saw a girl standing in the shadows, sipping a beaker of wine. Her left arm was wrapped in linen bandages, all the way from her wrist to her elbow.

'Tiya! There you are. These are the dancers from Waset, Mut and Isis,' said Heria. 'And this is Tiya.'

Tiya smiled, but her smile was brief. 'Welcome to Set Maat,' she said.

'Heria told me that you're a dancer, too,' said Isis. 'I'm so sorry about your arm.'

Tiya glanced down at her bandages. 'Thank you. It's beginning to heal, I think.'

'How did you hurt it?' asked Mut.

'I fell down the courtyard steps.' Tiya spoke quickly, then looked away, as if she didn't want to talk about it.

She's unhappy, thought Isis suddenly, seeing how her shoulders sagged.

Mut didn't seem to have noticed. 'I like your bracelet,' she said, pointing at Tiya's good arm, which was adorned with a beautiful gold bracelet inlaid with precious lapis lazuli.

'Oh!' Tiya looked flustered. She shook the bracelet, so that it glinted in the firelight. 'Thank you. My brother gave it to me.'

There was a brief silence. Isis noticed that Heria was staring at the gold band, her eyes wide. Tiya returned her gaze anxiously.

Then Heria stepped forward, and spoke in her friend's ear. Hurriedly, Tiya tried to take off the bracelet, then winced with pain. Her friend reached and removed it for her.

'Don't be so foolish,' Isis heard Heria mutter. 'Keep it somewhere safe.'

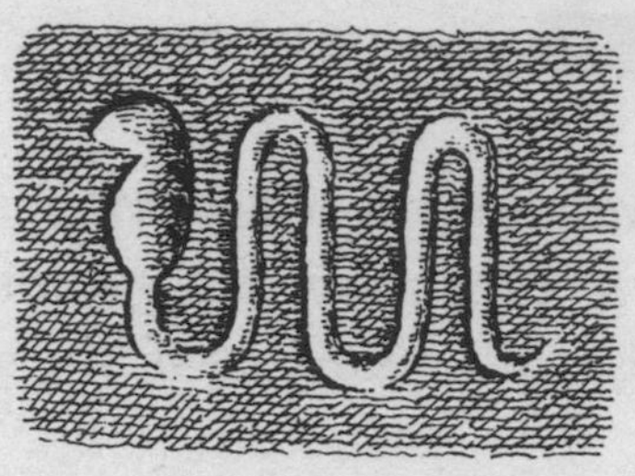

CHAPTER FOUR

Hopi left the party long before it was over. The villagers were growing ever more boisterous, and few of them were interested in talking to a shy young stranger. Besides, he wanted to think. *Serqet. Meretseger*. New names, new gods, in a village full of mystery and knowledge . . . Its atmosphere filled him with longing. Tonight, even watching Isis made him feel miserable, for it reminded him of his own uselessness. He wandered the streets of the village, gazing up at the stars, until at last he grew tired and headed to the house of Khonsu to sink down on one of the beds.

When he woke, it was still dark in the little room. Sounds of breathing surrounded him; Isis, Mut and Heria must have crept in during the night. Quietly, he got up and went out to the courtyard, and found some water by the first glimmers of dawn. Refreshed, he left the house and gazed up at the mountain.

'Meretseger,' he whispered. *She who loves silence.* He had arranged to meet Seti again that morning, but not until the sun had advanced a little. There was time. For an instant, he thought of Rahotep's warning: *Do not follow strangers who may lead you into trouble.* But he wasn't following anyone; he was going to explore the mountainside for himself.

The path was steep. In places, it wound through narrow crevices; in others, it led dangerously close to the edge of the limestone cliffs. Sometimes, Hopi's dragging right leg caught on stones and pebbles, which rattled and clattered down behind him. Each time it happened he stopped, his heart pounding. But today, no one called out.

Soon, a magnificent view of the village began to unfold. Hopi stepped off the path and found himself a place to sit, overlooking the valley with its temples. He could just see the narrow sliver of the Nile in the distance.

He stiffened. Voices. Somewhere above, along the stony path. Hurriedly, he looked for a place to hide, and pressed himself against the ledge where he sat. He held his breath.

There was a boy. 'I d-d-don't want to die,' he hiccupped, his voice jarred by sobs and the speed at which they were marching down the path.

'Don't be stupid.' A mature man's voice, gruff and impatient.

'It's c-c-cursed,' wailed the boy. 'The goddess will k-kill us.'

Hopi tried to peer up, but he could see nothing. There was just the slap of sandals, very close now.

'It's not cursed. The first one was badly made and in the wrong place, that's all. I should have seen to it myself.'

'I don't want to go there again –'

'You'll do as you're told.'

The footsteps passed. A couple of limestone pebbles rolled past Hopi's shoulder. He peered out, and caught a glimpse of a young, anxious boy, and an older man whose face was familiar. He'd been at the party the night before, talking to Nakht. But that didn't mean much. *Everyone* had spoken to Nakht.

The pair moved on beyond a high boulder and down a steep section of path. Then they were gone. Hopi eased himself away from the ledge carefully, and listened. Nothing, no one else. He waited until there was total silence before setting off.

The sun had risen higher now, and was glancing

off the rocks. Hopi hurried down the path, past the village tomb-chapels, and spotted Seti waiting for him by the cemetery gate. He saw at once that the painter was angry.

'Where d'you think you've been?' Seti demanded.

'Sorry,' said Hopi. 'I woke up early, so I went for a walk, that's all.'

'You can't do that,' said Seti. 'You can't just *go for a walk*. Not here. I told you that yesterday.'

'Breakfast time!' Heria's voice broke into Isis's sleep. She turned over, trying not to hear it.

'Isis! Wake up!' It was Mut this time, and she couldn't ignore it.

She sat up and looked at the bed where her brother had been lying asleep the night before. It was empty. 'Where's Hopi?' she demanded.

Mut was sitting on the floor. She pulled a face. 'How should we know?'

Heria had prepared a bowl of dates and figs, and a little pile of flatbreads. 'It's yesterday's bread,' she said, 'but I've warmed it up on the embers in the oven.' She handed both Mut and Isis a piece, then bit into one herself. 'Does Hopi often go off on his own?' she asked.

'Well . . . I suppose so,' said Isis, rubbing her eyes.

'All the time,' said Mut, reaching for a fig. 'He goes off hunting for snakes and scorpions and horrible things like that.' She shuddered.

Heria frowned. 'Does he really?'

Isis felt a tight knot of guilt growing inside. For once, she hardly noticed Mut's comments. She'd been feeling bad ever since she'd failed to find Hopi the night before. Parties could be difficult for him sometimes. It wasn't much fun being left on his own while everyone else in the family was performing. And that strange man he'd been talking to . . . who was he? And why had her brother crept out so early in the morning?

'I should go and find him,' she said, swinging her legs off the bed.

Mut and Heria stared at her. 'Don't be crazy, Isis,' said Mut. 'He'll come back. What's so different about today?'

It was impossible to say, but Isis stood up. 'I just have to go,' she said.

'But you've no idea where he's gone!' exclaimed Mut.

Isis hesitated. It was true, but she clutched the amulet around her neck. 'The gods will show me.'

Heria put down her flatbread. Her face was full of concern. 'Isis, you can't go wandering off on your own,' she said. 'The village is guarded and full of spies.'

Isis met her gaze. 'Then Hopi definitely needs me,' she said.

'And what am I supposed to tell Mother and Father?' asked Mut, with a sly gleam in her eye.

'Don't tell them anything,' said Isis. 'He can't have gone far.'

There was a brief silence. Then Heria smiled at Isis, understanding in her eyes. 'Take water with you. Mut and I will wait for you here,' she said. 'If anyone comes to the door, I will tell them you're all still sleeping.' She placed a slight emphasis on *all*.

Isis smiled back. Mut wouldn't be running to Nefert and Paneb, thanks to Heria. She slipped on her rough linen day-dress, put her feet in her sandals and slung Heria's leather water pouch over her shoulder. Then she headed out on to the street, feeling glad, for the second time, that Heria was on her side.

Seti led the way up the mountain path. He still seemed to be in a bad mood, and Hopi was puzzled. Why should Seti care that he'd been for a walk on his own? He laboured after the painter, who climbed only a short distance before turning off, as he'd done the day before.

Hopi stopped. Once more, the words of Rahotep

echoed in his mind. *Do not follow strangers* . . . He still wasn't sure what the man had meant, but perhaps it was unwise to follow Seti, after all.

He nodded up at the mountain. 'I think we'd stand a better chance of finding cobras up there.'

Seti turned to face him. 'We're not going that way,' he said flatly.

'Why?' asked Hopi. 'I mean, I know it's forbidden, but as far as I can make out, I'm not supposed to leave the village at all. So what's the difference?'

The young painter folded his arms. 'You're being very awkward today.'

Hopi shrugged. 'I don't think so. I just don't know where you're leading me, that's all. You say you want to find a cobra, but I think there's more to it than that.'

Seti stepped closer. Suddenly, his eyes were full of fear. 'Why would you think that?' he demanded. 'What do you know?'

Hopi stepped backwards, shaking his head. 'Nothing . . . nothing much . . . but Rahotep said –'

'You've spoken to Rahotep!' Seti sounded anguished. He took another step, and now he seemed almost menacing.

'I've done nothing!' exclaimed Hopi, backing off further. 'All I've done is try to help you, and I don't even know what for!'

Seti was clenching and unclenching his fists. He seemed on the verge of losing control, and Hopi watched him carefully. But then he spotted something else, out of the corner of his eye.

It was a cobra.

The cobra's body was olive brown, with a dark patch on its head, and Hopi knew exactly what that meant. This cobra could spit, right into the eyes of its victim. Cornered on a ledge, its hood fully extended, it was ready to attack.

Hopi stood perfectly still, and averted his eyes.

'What is –' began Seti.

'Don't look,' ordered Hopi.

Seti opened his mouth to speak, and began to turn his head.

'DON'T look!' shouted Hopi.

Seti's face went rigid. Hopi's stern order glued him to the spot. Seconds ticked past.

'Walk towards me.'

Seti did as he said. One step, two . . . the snake saw its chance. It lowered its guard, slithered down the ledge and disappeared between the rocks.

Hopi relaxed. 'It's all right now. It's gone.'

Seti spun round, scanning the rocks. 'What's gone?'

'A cob—'

'NO!' The word burst from Seti like an explosion. 'We found a cobra and you didn't let me see it!'

'But if you'd looked it would have –'

Seti wouldn't let him finish. He had worked himself into a rage. 'You have no idea what this means!' he cried. 'Meretseger is not your goddess. You didn't even know who she is, and now you've interfered and stood between us. How dare you! How *dare* you!' He reached out and gave Hopi a shove.

Hopi nearly lost his balance. He staggered back, then turned and began to hobble up the mountain track. 'Look for cobras yourself!' he cried. 'I'm not helping you any more! I want nothing to do with you or your goddess!'

Seti stayed where he was. 'Go!' he shouted after Hopi. 'Go, and see what will become of you! May the mountain swallow you up and the goddess rain down her punishments upon you!'

Hopi struggled on, the words of the curse whirling around in his head.

Isis slipped quickly between the chapels of the cemetery, her slight form barely making a sound. She wasn't worried about being seen. One of her greatest skills was being able to melt into shadows and disappear. She gazed up at the mountain to assess her options. There was a pathway winding up beyond the cemetery, but it looked like a long way round. Apart from that, the cliff directly above the tombs sloped fairly gently, and there were plenty of footholds. Isis was nimble – she'd save time if she went straight up.

The first section was easy. But then came a slab of smooth, sand-blasted rock that was much steeper than it had looked from below. Isis took a deep breath, and dug her fingernails into a little crevice. Scraping her ankles and knees, she hauled herself up. This was harder than she had imagined. The sun was growing hotter, beating down on her head. She looked up. *Not far now,* she told herself. *Not far now . . .*

By the time she reached the top of the cliff, Isis was covered in grazes and white limestone dust. Nefert wouldn't be happy about that, she reflected, but what were a few grazes compared to Hopi's safety? She brushed herself down and clambered on. Along the way, she crossed the path, which zigzagged off to the right. Perhaps Hopi would have followed it; it might lead to the Great Place itself.

She hesitated for only a second, then took the path and trotted along it quickly, taking little leaps through the gullies and over jutting boulders. Soon she could see the Temples of a Million Years down in the valley and the view beyond them to the Nile. But she didn't stop. Hopi had to be here somewhere. Isis scanned the horizon constantly, but there was no sign of him. Her anxiety mounting, she began to run, leaping from rock to rock and calling for her brother.

Slowly, the pathway opened out. She was on a ridge, and to the left a vast desert landscape stretched on for ever: endless mountains and gullies, all made of bare, sun-parched rock. A strange sense of awe crept over Isis, and her knees began to tremble. Truly, people did not belong here. This was the Red Land, the land of the wild and dangerous god Seth, where people were carried to the Next World.

Some little huts came into view, and Isis approached them quietly. They seemed deserted. She crept up to them and peered inside. There was no one there, but there were signs of life – bits of leftover bread and a few grapes on a stalk that had been picked almost clean. Isis thought it over. These must be workmen's huts: this was where the men stayed when they were working on the tombs, to save the long walk back to the village every night.

She left the huts and walked to the edge of the ridge. Down below her was a dry, stony valley, its limestone gullies dotted with little sealed doors. She gasped.

They were the doors of tombs. It was the Great Place.

Isis knew at once that Hopi wouldn't have gone down there. It was a sacred place, protected by the kings' magic, and her brother would never take such a risk. It was also protected by guards – she noticed one slumped in the shade, and another wandering up and down, listless in the rising heat.

No. She would not find Hopi here; but with his bad leg she doubted he would have gone on further. She decided to backtrack, then left the path and skirted the Great Place to the south. The sun was hot now, and she was thirsty, but she wanted to save the little water she had. The sunlight was reflecting from the yellow-white rocks, the glare nearly blinding her, but she carried on, scanning every gully for the figure of her brother.

She began to lose track of time. Boulders seemed to loom up, then pass by on either side. Sometimes she could hear the slap-slap of her sandals on the stones; at others she could hear only her own hoarse, dry breathing. When she saw a dark gap in the shimmering brightness of a rocky gully, all she could think of was shade, and she headed towards it instinctively. It was only when she was a few metres away that she realised that Hopi was half-sitting, half-lying across its entrance.

Her throat was parched. 'Hopi,' she managed to croak.

His eyes were closed, but they flickered open at the sound of her voice.

'Isis,' he murmured. 'What are you doing here?'

Isis flung herself down and hugged him. 'I found you,' she said. 'I knew I would, I knew . . . You need water. I've brought some – here you are.' Hurriedly, she lifted the little water pouch from around her shoulders and pressed it to her brother's lips.

He drank gratefully, then handed the pouch back to Isis. 'Why?' he asked. 'Why did you come?'

Isis shook her head. 'I don't know,' she said. 'I was worried, that's all. There are strange things going on in the village.' And as they shared the rest of the water, Isis recounted everything that Heria had told her, and described the scene with the dancer Tiya, her broken arm and her bracelet.

Hopi listened quietly, letting the water do its work. When he had revived a little, he sat up and looked around. 'You were lucky to find me,' he said.

'Yes,' said Isis. 'But what are you doing here, anyway? What happened? I saw a man talking to you last night. You looked frightened. Then this morning, you'd gone.'

Hopi watched as a spiny-tailed lizard poked its

head out of a crevice, and ducked back into it. He thought of Seti's curse. 'I don't understand most of it, Isis. I've met a painter who wants to find cobras. We found one, but he didn't see it, so he grew angry and placed the curse of the mountain's goddess upon me.'

'The mountain's goddess? Who is she?' asked Isis.

'She's a cobra goddess. Her name is Meretseger,' said Hopi. 'And the man who spoke to me last night also gave me a warning. He said that the mountain is a sacred place and that I shouldn't follow strangers here. I wished I'd listened to him, now.'

'And that is all the man said?'

'No,' said Hopi. 'He told me about another goddess. Serqet. Have you heard of her?'

Isis shook her head. 'I don't think so.'

'He said the gods show themselves when they're ready. Something like that. I'm not sure I fancy meeting one of them up here.'

A breeze stirred the air, bringing a little relief from the scorching sun. Isis looked up at the brilliant blue of the sky against the rocks, and began to feel that the place was somehow peaceful.

'I think you should forget that curse,' she said. She gestured around them. The dark fissure in the rocks where they sat offered deep, cool shade. 'This cobra goddess can't be so terrible. Even in the heat of the day, she has given us shelter.'

Both of them glanced into the fissure, which seemed to continue behind a big boulder. Hopi shuffled back, and leaned against it. To his surprise, he felt the boulder shift. He peered around it, and allowed his eyes to adjust to the darkness. Isis moved closer, and poked her head through the gap, too. It was then, looking closely at the sides of the walls, that they saw the truth. This might have been a natural opening in the rocks – at first. But beyond the boulder, there were marks: the scorings and scrapings of chisels. It had been widened by human hands. It was a tunnel.

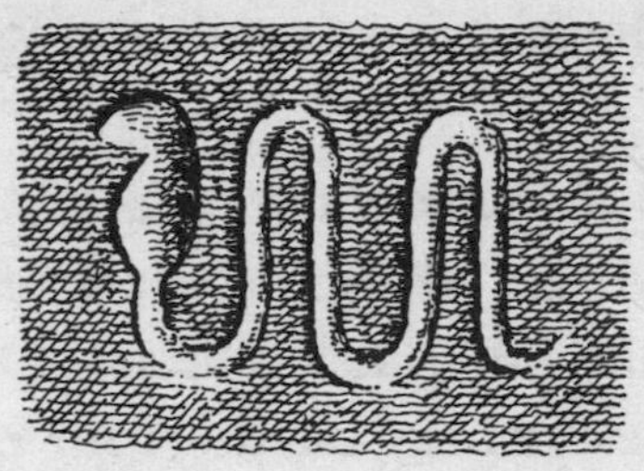

CHAPTER FIVE

Isis and Hopi pulled their heads back into the daylight and stared at each other.

'Do you think it's a tomb?' whispered Isis.

'Can't be,' said Hopi. 'We're nowhere near the village cemetery.'

'But . . . what about the Great Place?' asked Isis. 'I saw it earlier. I think it must be quite close.' She peered up at the mountainside uncertainly. She had become so disorientated when she was hunting for Hopi that she couldn't be sure how far she had walked.

Hopi shook his head. 'Not a chance. Look at the tunnel, Isis. It's just a narrow gap in the rocks. It's tiny. You couldn't get anyone's coffin through there, let alone a royal one. And it's not even sealed.'

Isis crawled forward and examined the tunnel again. 'I could get through there easily enough, though,' she said. She paused. 'Shall I try?'

Curiosity was burning inside Hopi, but the voice of his father echoed around his head . . . *Look after Isis* . . . What if something happened to her? He couldn't possibly allow her to go on her own.

'We'll both go,' he said.

Isis frowned. 'What about your leg?'

Hopi shifted it impatiently. 'All we need to do is crawl,' he said. 'I think I can manage that.'

'But . . .' Isis was thinking. 'It's so dark in there. We won't be able to see.'

It was a good point. Hopi reached for his bag again. They would have to make a light somehow. Whoever made the tunnel would have had oil lamps to work by, but they had nothing like that.

'I have my tinder-sticks,' said Hopi, rummaging through his bag. 'But we've nothing to make a lamp, or a torch.'

'Then we'll have to explore in the darkness,' said Isis, sounding braver than she felt.

'Then what? We won't be able to see what we find.' Hopi looked around, and spotted a few bone-dry acacia twigs lying amongst the rocks. Struggling to his feet, he quickly gathered a handful.

Isis grasped his idea. 'Could you make a spark in the darkness?' she asked. 'Just by feel?'

'I think so, if there's enough space. It depends what we find. If we don't reach anything, we'll just have to crawl out backwards.'

'We can do that.' Isis felt her heart beating a little faster. 'I'll lead the way. It'll be easier for me, because I'm smaller.'

Hopi nodded. 'All right, then. Check the tunnel as you go,' he instructed. 'Stop if you get scared. I'll be right behind you.'

They looked into each other's eyes. Impulsively, Isis gave Hopi a hug. Then she bent down once more and began to grope her way along the narrow tunnel.

With Hopi blocking the light behind her, the tunnel was soon completely dark. Isis could see nothing ahead, not even the slightest glimmer of reflected light. It was as though her eyes had stopped working. Fighting back her fear, she felt the walls and roof of the tunnel with her fingers before pulling herself forward.

'Keep going,' Hopi's voice reassured her. 'I'm right here.'

Isis wanted to stop. It was difficult to breathe, and she had never known such total blackness. The tunnel seemed to wind on for ever into the depths of the mountain. But every now and again, Hopi's hand touched her heels and gave her courage.

The air was changing. It seemed colder, and was mingled with faint odours that Isis could vaguely recognise. Old wood, perhaps, and incense. She groped upwards for the roof ahead of her and suddenly found it had gone. Reaching out, she traced her hand around the edge of the tunnel. The walls had gone, too. Wherever it was leading, the tunnel had finally arrived.

Isis checked the floor ahead. There was no drop below. She wriggled out into the space, and found that she could stretch her arms. She reached as high as she could, and touched nothing. Her heart pounding, she tried standing up.

'Hopi!' she called in excitement. 'It's huge!'

'Stay where you are!' called her brother, still deep inside the tunnel. 'I'm almost there.'

Isis did as he said. It was spooky, standing in the middle of such darkness. Even here, there were no chinks of light for her eyes to grasp and adjust to. When Hopi reached the open space, only her ears told her he was there. She listened as he fumbled with his bag, arranged the little acacia twigs and began to rub the tinder-sticks together.

Chapter Five

There was a sudden flare of light as the sticks made a spark, which caught on the dry acacia. Isis and Hopi both gasped. By the flickering flame, images of all the gods stared down from the walls around them. It *was* a royal tomb! It couldn't be anything else. A huge stone sarcophagus stood in the centre of the chamber, and all around them were beautiful, priceless objects.

But many of them were not in one piece.

'It's been ransacked!' exclaimed Isis. 'Look . . . look at that chair – it's almost been hacked to bits!'

All that was left was the wood, scraped clean of its gold plate and precious inlays. Only little flecks remained to show that it had once been covered. Chariot wheels lay in a crooked pile against the wall, and a painted statue of the god Anubis lay thrown on its side on the floor. They gazed around in disbelief. Anything that could fit into the little tunnel had clearly been taken.

The acacia twigs had almost burnt out. The flames were already sinking to ash and ember. In less than a minute, they would be engulfed in darkness once more.

'This is a terrible place,' said Isis, her voice trembling. 'Hopi, we have to get out of here, before the gods seek their vengeance!'

Hopi nodded his agreement. His chest felt tight

with anger. He poked at the acacia twigs to create one more flare of light, and took a final look around. The last thing he saw was a dark hole in one corner, not far from the tunnel they had come through.

'There's another hole there,' he said, but Isis had already disappeared, and was crawling towards daylight. The acacia fire died, and Hopi stood alone in the darkness.

Isis had never been so glad to see the sun. She emerged from the tunnel blinking, almost weak with relief, then immediately turned and peered back down it.

'Hopi!' she called. 'Are you coming?'

'Yes,' her brother's voice came back. 'But my leg hurts. I have to go slowly.'

Isis sat down to wait. Her stomach rumbled, and suddenly she realised that she hadn't eaten since early that morning. She glanced up at the sun. It was beginning to dip towards the west. She was sure that Heria would have done her best to protect them, but now they'd been gone for hours. No one would believe they'd slept until the afternoon. They were going to be in big trouble.

'Come on, Hopi!' she called, a little anxiously. 'It's getting late!'

Chapter Five

When Hopi's head poked out of the tunnel at last, his face was pinched with pain. The hard rock had scraped his bad leg several times. He hauled himself out.

'Look at the sun,' said Isis. 'It's mid-afternoon. We have to get back to the village. I'm not even sure where it is, though.'

Hopi gritted his teeth and stood up. 'It's that way,' he said, pointing. 'It's not as far as you think. We'll be all right, Isis. But you mustn't say a word to anyone, d'you understand?'

Isis had already imagined telling Heria, or even Mut. She could just picture their faces. And anyway, it was going to be tricky, explaining where they'd been. 'Why not?'

Hopi thought of the man and boy he'd seen that morning. He thought of Rahotep's warning, and Seti's anger. 'We don't know who to trust,' he said, setting off up the gully.

'We can trust Heria,' said Isis.

'No, we can't,' said Hopi, wincing with each step that he took. 'You told me yourself that she made Tiya hide her bracelet. What if it came from this tomb?'

Isis said nothing. She was sure that Heria wouldn't have anything to do with tomb-robbing. She just *knew*. But maybe Hopi was right – they couldn't say anything yet. She took her brother's arm to support him as he walked, and, thanks to his sense of direction, they made their way slowly to the path.

'Do you realise just how much trouble you've caused?' demanded Nefert, her eyes flashing. 'Nakht sent men out to search for you not long after noon. He's an important man and he has much better things to do than hunt for his guests!'

Isis and Hopi stood with their heads bowed. 'Sorry, Nefert,' murmured Isis. 'We got lost.'

'But what were you doing up there in the first place? That's what I want to know!' Nefert's anger wasn't spent yet. 'If it was anything to do with this dreadful obsession with reptiles . . .' She shook her head in anger and disgust. 'Well, was it?'

Hopi bit his lip. He had been on the verge of saying they were looking for snakes. Now he thought better of it. 'We were just exploring,' he said. 'We went up to look at the view.'

'A likely story.' Nefert folded her arms. 'Now I want to make something clear. Paneb and I have offered you both a home for almost a year. For the most part, I'm pleased with your progress, Isis. But last night I was not impressed. You weren't concentrating at all.'

Isis felt her heart plummet. So Nefert had seen her mistake, after all.

'Making mistakes is simply not acceptable. We are a professional troupe. And just look at you now! You're covered in scrapes and grazes, yet you know very well that you're performing again tomorrow night. What sort of dancer gets herself into such a mess?'

Nefert paused, letting her words sink in. Then she carried on, lowering her voice. 'We can't afford to keep you for nothing. If you are not going to take your dancing seriously, you may have to move elsewhere. Especially as I'm not sure I want a snake-lover in the household.'

It was horrible. Isis felt her knees tremble in shock. She looked appealingly at Paneb, but his eyes were trained on the ground. He and Nefert must have discussed this. He wouldn't allow his wife to say things she didn't mean.

Hopi put an arm around his sister's shoulders. 'Isis is a talented dancer,' he said. 'Don't punish her because of me. I have already promised that I will never bring a snake to the house again.'

Paneb raised his eyes and regarded them both calmly. 'You are always quick to defend your sister, Hopi,' he said. 'This is only natural, and good. But you must remember that we have our concerns about you. You must not lead Isis astray.'

Isis wanted to protest. It all felt so unfair. Nefert and Paneb had no idea what was happening right under their noses. What were a few cuts and grazes and a harmless snake or two compared to the robbery of a royal tomb? She opened her mouth to speak, but Hopi immediately squeezed her shoulder hard, in warning. She closed her mouth again: there was nothing she could do.

Hopi felt exhausted, but he couldn't sleep. It had been a miserable evening. He and Isis had had to sit quietly, on their best behaviour, in the house of Amen-Kha, the boring draughtsman who was hosting Nefert and Paneb. Now they were back in the house of Khonsu, getting an early night in preparation for the second party.

Hopi lay on his back and stared upwards, but it wasn't the ceiling he saw. There were too many other images in his mind's eye: Seti and the cobra; Rahotep with his warning and strange talk of Serqet; Isis with her tale of Tiya and her beautiful gold bracelet. And the tomb . . . the ransacked tomb, left in disarray with its precious objects stripped clean. None of it made any sense.

And then there was the family. Hopi's heart filled with anger and dread. Would he and Isis really have to return to the life they'd known before? Limping around with nothing but a begging bowl?

The girls were already asleep. Hopi turned on his side and curled into a ball. At last he drifted off.

It seemed only minutes before something was waking him up.

'Hopi!'

He opened his eyes. A young boy was shaking his shoulder, panic written over his face.

'Seti is calling for you!'

Hopi sat up. He saw, to his astonishment, that it was already dawn. 'Seti?'

'He's been attacked by a snake!' jabbered the boy. 'I heard him screaming on the mountain so I ran up and he was calling for you. "The visitor! Hopi the visitor!" he was screaming. I didn't know who you were, but someone told me you were staying here.'

Hopi didn't need to hear any more. With a sick feeling in his stomach, he knew exactly what had happened. As the girls stirred and muttered in their sleep, he leaped up, ran to the courtyard and grabbed the first full flagon he could find.

'Take me to him,' he instructed the boy. 'Hurry, and help me carry this!'

They half-ran, half-hobbled out into the early morning sun and headed straight for the cemetery gate. Hopi could already hear Seti's screams, echoing against the rocks. He was not the only one. The households near the gate had been aroused, and people were hurrying out to find the source of the commotion.

'Call Rahotep!' someone cried.

Hopi and the boy carried the flagon between them, gasping for breath as they climbed up between the chapel courtyards. Seti was staggering towards them from the mountain path, blinded, his screams a terrible sound.

'Lie down!' Hopi shouted. 'Lie down and put your head back!'

Seti slumped to the ground, scraping at his eyes with his hands. They were hardly visible. The flesh around them had swollen horribly, and Hopi caught a glimpse of whites that had turned to fiery scarlet.

'Keep your hands away!' he instructed. He splashed the contents of the flagon into Seti's face, then stared in dismay. It wasn't a water flagon. It was beer! Too bad: it was all he had. He kept sloshing the fluid into Seti's eyes as the painter tossed and turned his head, spluttering as beer went up his nose.

Hopi kept going. 'Keep *still*!' he ordered desperately.

His arms were aching from the weight of the flagon, but Hopi knew he had to use all the beer he had. He had to flood Seti's eyes with it until there was nothing left. When the last drop had gone, he looked around at the crowd that had gathered, staring at the scene open-mouthed.

Seti had stopped screaming, but now he was weeping, tears pouring down his face from between the swollen slits.

'Can you see anything?' asked Hopi.

'No . . . no . . . she has blinded me . . . Meretseger has blinded me!' Seti wailed.

There were murmurs in the crowd:

'She has spoken. Blindness is always her vengeance. This is how she makes herself heard.'

'Who is this boy? Where is Rahotep?'

'He is coming. He is on his way.'

Hopi studied Seti's face, feeling anguish inside. He could guess exactly what had happened. Seti had returned to the spot where they had found the cobra, and waited for it to reappear. He had looked at it in defiance of Hopi's advice. And now, he might never see again.

The anger of Meretseger was indeed terrible.

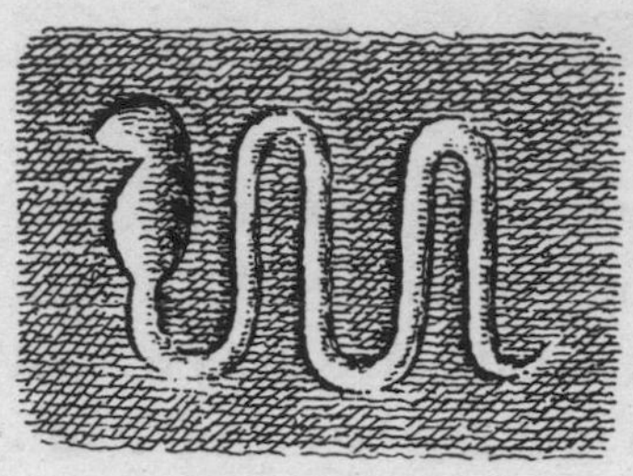

CHAPTER SIX

'Rahotep is coming!'

A cry went up at the cemetery gate. Hopi was baffled. Rahotep was the man he'd met at the party. What had he got to do with this? The crowd parted to make way for the priest of Serqet. Rahotep hurried up, bleary-eyed, and surveyed the scene. A clamour of voices told him what had happened, as Hopi waited by Seti's side.

'Meretseger has spoken!' people shouted.

'The goddess has punished him!'

'He is blinded!'

'The Peak of the West has been angered!'

Rahotep took in Seti's bloated face and eyes, his drenched tunic and the empty flagon at Hopi's feet. He looked at Hopi. 'Did you do this?' he demanded,

gesturing at the sticky fluid everywhere.

'Yes,' said Hopi. 'I know this snake – it is a cobra, the one that spits. I thought I had brought water to throw into his eyes, but beer is better than nothing.'

Rahotep knelt down by Seti's side. Gently, he prised each eye open in turn, as Seti yelped in pain. Then he stood up and addressed the crowd. 'Take him to my home!' he ordered. 'He needs herbs and magic. Hurry!'

Village boys rushed forward to grab Seti's arms and legs. They hoisted him up on to their shoulders and set off, jogging him down through the cemetery and towards the gate with most of the villagers in tow. Hopi stayed where he was, and watched them go.

Rahotep also stood still. 'Who told you about this cobra that spits?' he asked.

Hopi shrugged. 'No one. I've seen them before, that's all.'

'So who taught you what to do?'

'I have no teacher. All I knew was that Seti had venom in his eyes and that it must be washed out.'

'Then it is indeed a gift,' murmured Rahotep. Hopi frowned, wondering what he meant, but the priest was already striding down the mountain.

'Come to my home later today,' he called over his shoulder. 'Any of the villagers will tell you where it is.'

Isis, Mut and Heria rushed out of the house just in time to see Seti being carried along the street with a crowd of villagers running after him.

'What's happened?' cried Heria.

A chorus of excited voices answered her: *The revenge of Meretseger! The goddess had blinded him! A massive, terrible cobra with venom in its tongue! The visitor Hopi with a flagon of beer* . . . a web of garbled stories spilled out.

Heria burst into tears. 'I can't believe it,' she sobbed. 'First Tiya and now Seti. And on the day of Baki's party! Why is the goddess so angry? Why?'

Isis put an arm around her. She didn't know what to say.

'We must go to Baki's house,' hiccupped Heria. 'This is a sign. Surely he will have to cancel his party tonight.'

Cancel the party! Isis was dismayed. If it didn't go ahead, the dance troupe had no reason to stay. They would have to leave and head back to Waset. But she and Hopi had only just discovered the tunnel – and the royal tomb! They couldn't possibly just go without getting to the root of it all.

'We must wait for Hopi,' Isis said. 'I want to hear what happened from him.'

They found Hopi limping down from the cemetery. He told them everything that had happened. 'But I don't know why everyone called for Rahotep,' he finished.

'Rahotep?' said Heria. 'Of course they called for him. He's Seti's only hope.' And her tears welled up again.

The others looked at each other blankly.

'Why?' asked Mut.

'You don't know?' Heria sniffed. 'The priest of Serqet heals the bites of snakes and scorpions. Now come, we must hurry.' And she led them off towards the house of Baki.

Isis, Mut and Hopi trailed after her. Isis was trying to piece together everything she had heard. Wasn't Rahotep the man that Hopi had met at the party? The one who had warned him against exploring the mountain?

They arrived at Baki's house only to find a guard posted outside. News of Seti's misfortune had travelled fast, and Heria was not the only one to realise what it might mean. Everyone wanted to know whether Baki's party would go ahead, and the guard's job was to turn people away.

'Baki is meeting with some of the elders now. They will speak to the village later,' was all he would say.

'So my father Khonsu is there!' exclaimed Heria.

The guard nodded. 'Yes.'

'Then I want to see him,' demanded Heria. 'Tell him I'm here with a group of our guests. They need to know what is happening, surely you can see that?'

The guard hesitated. He disappeared inside for a few moments, then came back and opened the door wider. 'You can go in,' he said.

Isis, Mut and Hopi followed Heria into the house. She stopped outside the front room and stood respectfully in the doorway to speak to her father. Isis and Hopi both edged closer to peer over her shoulder. Inside the room, four of the village elders sat around in a circle. Isis knew two of them – Nakht, the foreman who had held the last party, and Heria's father Khonsu, the chief scribe. Then there was a man she guessed must be Baki, and another with his back to them. There was a young servant, too, serving them sweet pastries.

'Heria. You should not be here,' said Khonsu. 'But as you are, I have a job for you. You must deliver a message.'

'Yes, Father,' said Heria. 'Who to?'

'When the goddess strikes, we must listen,' said Nakht, his voice grave. 'We dare not anger her further. You must tell our visitors that tonight's party cannot go ahead.'

'Go at once,' said Baki, dismissing them with a wave of his hand. 'Leave us. We have many things to discuss.'

Isis felt her heart sink. So it was true. They would have to go back to Waset, without solving any of the mysteries. Nefert and Paneb would be disappointed, too, because they would be paid for only one party. A ripple of fear passed through her as she remembered Nefert's words: *We can't afford to keep you for nothing . . .* The less work they had, the less they would want to keep a dancer who made mistakes.

They turned to leave. It was only as they stepped back out into the street that Isis noticed Hopi's expression. Her brother's face was frozen in shock.

Hopi was still trying to take it all in. That boy who had served the sweet pastries . . . Hopi would recognise his face anywhere – and that of his master, too.

'What is it? What is it?' Isis whispered.

Hopi shook his head, mute. He didn't dare speak in front of Heria and Mut. The man he had seen on the mountain the day before was none other than

Foreman Baki. But what could it possibly mean? It didn't make sense.

They hurried back up the main street to the house where Paneb and Nefert were staying, and Heria banged on the door.

Nefert and Paneb were sitting on the floor with their hosts and their two young boys, eating breakfast. Mut rushed to Nefert, and flung herself into her arms.

'Mother, the party's been cancelled!' she cried.

'Cancelled?' Nefert and Paneb spoke at once.

'One of the village men has been attacked by a cobra!' Mut buried her head on Nefert's shoulder. 'They say there's a fearful cobra goddess, and she's angry with everyone, and they're all afraid of her vengeance . . . it's horrible. I don't like it here, Mother. I want to go home!'

'A cobra!' Nefert's voice was sharp, and she immediately looked at Hopi. 'You didn't have anything to do with this, I hope?'

'No! No. I mean, I knew what had happened . . .' Hopi was aghast.

'He did.' Mut sat up again. 'He knew all about it before we did! He said it was a spitting snake and he was out there doing things with a flagon of beer, everyone saw him –' Mut's eyes were wild and accusatory.

Hopi's heart went cold. It was no use. He was going to have to accept the truth: the family would not tolerate him and his interests.

'I was doing no harm. I was trying to help,' he said quietly, but he didn't expect anyone to listen.

There was silence. Then Paneb looked around at the row of faces. 'Who told you that the party has been cancelled?' he asked.

'Nakht himself, sir,' said Heria. 'He and Baki and my father sent us to tell you.'

'Then there is nothing more to be said. We shall leave at once.' Paneb got to his feet and turned to his hosts. 'We are grateful for your hospitality, but these troubles are nothing to do with us. We shall pack our belongings and head back to Waset before noon.'

Hopi looked at Nefert, who was still clutching Mut close to her. What was she thinking? Would she ever truly accept him? It seemed less likely with every day that passed.

'Isis, Hopi, go and tell Sheri and Kia what has happened,' Paneb instructed them. 'I will go and fetch Happy from his tethering post. I want everyone to gather their belongings and be ready to leave as soon as possible.'

Hopi and Isis turned and left the house. As soon as they were outside, Isis tugged on Hopi's arm.

'So what was it?' she demanded. 'What did you see in Baki's house?'

But Hopi wouldn't answer. What did any of it matter? His heart was heavy, for he was sure that their days with the family were numbered. He and Isis would have to return to begging on the streets. Foreman Baki was not his concern.

'Nothing,' he muttered, and started limping up the street.

'Hopi! You saw something! I *know* you did.' Isis skipped alongside him. She lowered her voice. 'We can't leave the village now. We know too much.'

'And what will we live on if we stay?' asked Hopi, his voice bitter. 'Tell me, Isis. Will we live on the air, or the earth between the rocks?'

They reached the house where Sheri and Kia were staying, and knocked.

Back at Heria's house it had taken Isis five minutes to gather together her things. She had very few. Hopi had even fewer, and had gone to say goodbye to Seti and Rahotep. Mut had stayed behind to help Nefert with the two boys; once she came back to the house of Khonsu for her own things, it would be time to leave.

With her little linen bag at her feet, Isis sat down with Heria to wait.

'I wish you weren't going,' said Heria. 'I'm going to miss you.'

'I wish I wasn't going, either,' said Isis glumly. It was so frustrating. She was dying to tell Heria all about the tomb, but she didn't dare. Instead, she thought about the bracelet on Tiya's arm. As Hopi had said, it could have come from the royal tomb. It certainly looked like it. She thought for a moment. Asking questions couldn't do any harm, could it?

'Heria,' she said, 'where did Tiya get that bracelet she was wearing?'

Heria's eyes flew wide open. 'What bracelet?'

'She was wearing a gold bracelet at the party,' said Isis. 'You told her to take it off.'

'Oh, yes. I'd forgotten you'd seen it.' Heria looked frightened. 'You won't tell anyone about it, will you?'

Isis leaned forward. 'Why? What's the big secret?'

'I don't know,' Heria whispered. 'I don't know what Father's been investigating, but I think it's got something to do with the royal tombs.'

Isis couldn't resist. 'You think the bracelet was stolen?' she suggested.

Heria nodded. 'Yes. I think one of the tombs has been robbed. I can't believe that Tiya had anything to do with it but . . . I told her to hide it anyway.'

'But didn't you ask her where she got it?' demanded

Isis. '*I* would have done.'

'Of course I did.' Heria looked hurt. 'She just says the same thing every time.'

'I remember. She said it was a gift from her brother,' Isis recalled.

'Yes. And now Meretseger has punished Seti,' said Heria, her big eyes looking sad and thoughtful. 'So I don't know what to think. I hate to think that either of them would do anything wrong.'

'But what's Seti got to do with Tiya?' asked Isis.

Now Heria's eyes filled with astonishment. 'You don't know?' she exclaimed. 'It was Seti who gave Tiya the bracelet. *He's* her brother, of course!'

The rich smell of onions was everywhere. It was the first thing that struck Hopi as he entered Rahotep's house. Then he saw them, too – strings of onions hanging from doorways, and a whole sack by the side of the storeroom.

A servant showed him to the back of the house. 'You must stay very quiet and watch. Do not interrupt,' he instructed Hopi.

Hopi peered into the back room, which was lined with pots and jars and yet more onions; herbs were piled in one corner. A strange scene was beginning to unfold. Seti lay on the floor, his face wrapped in linen bandages; by his side lay a beaker of liquid and a large bowl. Rahotep stood over him, his arms outspread, chanting an incantation with his eyes shut.

'Flow out, poison! Come forth,' he intoned. 'Horus will cast you out. He will spit you out and punish you. Flow out, poison! Flow out!'

He bent down and touched Seti's bandaged eyes, then stood and chanted again. 'Come forth! Cast yourself upon the ground. This is not your place. Flow out, poison! Flow out!'

Suddenly, Seti sat up, his stomach heaving. Quick as a striking snake, Rahotep reached for the bowl and placed it in front of his patient. When he had finished vomiting, Seti lay back down with a groan.

Rahotep turned, and saw Hopi in the doorway. 'Welcome,' he said. He bent down to pick up the bowl and the beaker. 'Come, we will go to the courtyard now. The potion has done its work. Seti can rest.'

He led the way outside, handing the bowl to a servant. The beaker, however, he handed to Hopi. 'Taste it,' he said.

Hopi sniffed it first. Strong, acrid smells repelled him, and he jerked back.

'Go on,' Rahotep encouraged him. 'I want you to tell me what is in it.'

Gingerly, Hopi took a sip. 'Onions,' he said. 'Many

of them. Beer, and salt. And something I don't recognise.' He handed the beaker back. The liquid was foul.

Rahotep smiled. 'The taste you cannot place is the *sam*-plant,' he said. 'But otherwise, well done. This potion makes the victim vomit, as you have seen.'

Hopi was intrigued, but also puzzled. Why was Rahotep telling him all this?

'Thank you for showing me, sir,' he said. 'But the party of Baki has been cancelled, and we have no reason to stay. I just wanted to see Seti before I go.' He hesitated. 'Will he ever get his sight back, do you think?'

'That rests in the hands of the gods. Or the goddesses, I should say,' said Rahotep. He put a hand on Hopi's shoulder. 'I have done all I can. But you did more.'

Hopi blushed. He looked away, and spotted a statue of a woman in the corner of the courtyard, with the figure of a scorpion carved on her head. 'Is that a statue of Serqet, sir?' he asked.

'It is.'

Hopi felt drawn to the little statue, and stepped forward to look at it more closely. Its eyes seemed to meet his gaze, and he felt a warm tingle run up and down his spine.

'Do you still have your amulet?' enquired Rahotep.

'Yes, of course.' Hopi patted his linen bag, where the faience scorpion lay resting in its depths.

The priest of Serqet smiled. 'You did not receive it by chance,' he said.

Hopi felt his heart beat a little faster. 'Then how?'

'You have been chosen by the goddess to be one of her servants,' answered the priest. 'Of this I am more than sure.'

Hopi's mouth dropped open. A servant of the goddess Serqet? But he had only just heard of her. 'How . . . what . . .' he stuttered.

But now Rahotep raised a hand to silence him. He was listening – listening to a commotion that was growing outside. Hopi heard it, too: footsteps and the babble of many voices. They drew closer, closer . . . then came a hammering on the front door.

The servant reappeared. 'Shall I open it, sir?' he asked Rahotep.

'Of course, of course.'

Rahotep moved to where he could see the door. Curious, Hopi stood behind him. When it opened, his eyes widened: this was a serious visit indeed. Outside on the street stood Nakht, Baki and Khonsu, surrounded by a retinue of guards.

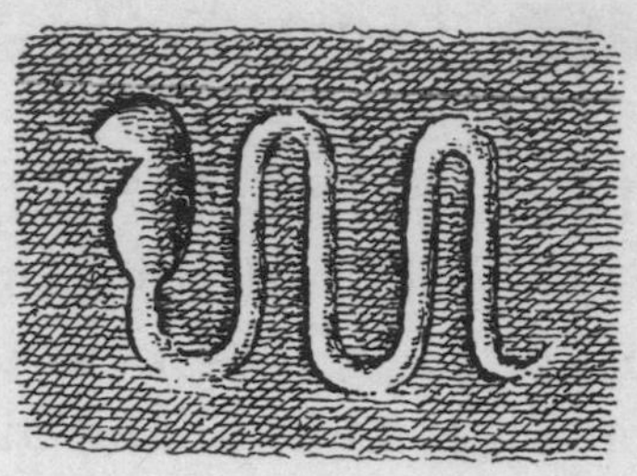

CHAPTER SEVEN

Isis was still reeling from the news. Seti and Tiya . . . brother and sister. Tiya's broken arm . . . the cobra's attack on Seti . . . and the golden bracelet that must have come from *somewhere*. Surely they had to be guilty? But Heria seemed so upset at the thought of it that Isis could find nothing to say.

'Isis, we have to go.' It was Mut, standing in the doorway. 'Everyone is ready. Where's Hopi?'

Isis stood up reluctantly. 'He's at the house of Rahotep,' she said.

'You mean the snake man?' Mut frowned. 'What's he doing there?'

'He went to see Seti.'

Mut's face darkened. 'Why would he want to see a man who's been punished by the gods? Why can't he just leave it all alone?'

It was too much for Isis. 'Why can't *you* try to understand him for once?'

Mut stalked into the room and snatched up her few belongings. 'I don't want to understand him. I hate snakes and I hate scorpions. So does Mother. You heard what she said.'

Isis felt as though Mut had hit her, hard, in the middle of her stomach.

'We're going,' Mut carried on. 'Mother and Father are waiting for us. They want to leave *now*. If you don't come and meet us quickly we'll just leave you here.'

Isis felt fury flare up. 'And that's exactly what you want, isn't it?' she cried. 'You want to get rid of us. You've wanted it right from the start! You hate Hopi and you hate me, too! Go on, then! Go! Leave us here!' She grabbed her linen bag. 'Hopi and I have looked after ourselves before. We'll do it again, if we have to!' And she ran out into the street with sobs rising in her throat.

She ran towards the main gate along the busy street where villagers stood outside their houses, sweeping their doorways and gossiping.

'Please,' asked Isis, stopping briefly to address an elderly woman, 'where is the house of Rahotep?'

'At the end, dear,' replied the woman, pointing. 'Last house before the gate.'

'Thank you,' Isis gulped, and set off again, dodging people as she ran. For some reason, a crowd had gathered outside the house of Rahotep. Breathless, she began to wriggle her way through until she could see the door. But then she stopped. The door was firmly shut, and two stern guards stood on either side of it.

The three village elders gathered around the priest of Serqet.

'We have come to see the painter Seti,' said Khonsu.

'I know,' replied Rahotep. 'But you are too early. He needs to rest.'

'We'll see him anyway.' Baki jerked his head towards Hopi. 'And get rid of this boy.'

Rahotep regarded him calmly. 'I cannot do that,' he said. 'That boy's destiny is intertwined with that of Seti. He must stay.'

The three men looked at each other. 'He can't do any harm,' said Nakht.

Baki shrugged. 'I suppose not.'

'Take us to Seti,' ordered Khonsu, turning back to the priest.

Rahotep had no choice. He led the way into the

back room where Seti lay still in the cool, dim light. He seemed to be asleep, but as the men gathered around him, he spoke.

'Who's there?' the painter asked in a hoarse voice.

'Can you hear me clearly?' asked Rahotep.

Seti licked his lips. 'Yes. But I am thirsty.' With a struggle, he sat up.

Rahotep fetched a beaker of water, and placed it to Seti's lips. 'The elders of the village are here,' he said. 'They wish to talk to you.'

With groping fingers, Seti felt the bandages across his eyes. 'What do they want?' he whispered. 'Is it not enough that I am blind?'

Foreman Nakht kneeled down beside him, and spoke in a voice that was surprisingly gentle. 'Why do you think you are blind?' he asked. 'What have you done to anger the goddess?'

Seti sat very still. His mouth moved, silently. Then, at last, he mumbled some words.

'Tiya . . . because of Tiya.'

'*Tiya?* Your sister?' Nakht looked up, a puzzled frown on his face.

'I put her in danger.' Seti's voice was faint.

Hopi wasn't sure what he'd expected to hear, but it wasn't this. And from the faces of the men, he could see it didn't make sense to them, either. He thought quickly. *Tiya . . . Tiya.* Wasn't she the dancer that Isis had told him about – the one with a golden bracelet?

Baki folded his arms. 'He's making it up,' he said.

'No . . . no,' protested Seti. 'Her arm is broken and I am being punished for that.'

Baki gave a humourless laugh. 'Your sister's arm has nothing to do with this.'

Hopi stared at Baki. He took in the bulky frame and the noble posture, the stiff line to his lip; he listened to the hard, gruff edge to his voice . . . *It's definitely him,* he thought to himself. His sense of shock returned, for there was no escaping it: Baki had been up to something on the mountain. But he was one of the most powerful men in the village; Nakht and Khonsu clearly trusted him completely. So who was Hopi to question or interfere?

Isis ran up to the guards outside Rahotep's door. 'Please, let me in,' she begged. 'My brother Hopi is in there.'

The guards shook their heads. 'Impossible,' they said. 'Strict orders. No one can enter.'

'But I have to see him,' begged Isis. Tears began to flow down her cheeks. 'Please. He's in there, I know he is.'

The guards shifted uncomfortably and looked

embarrassed. 'Nothing we can do,' said one. 'Orders from Foreman Nakht himself.'

Isis felt like kicking his shins. Some of the villagers gathered around her, coaxing her away from the guards.

'You can't go against the word of the foremen,' a woman told her.

'Where's the rest of your family?' asked another. 'Where's that pretty sister of yours?'

At the mention of her *pretty sister*, Isis wanted to howl with rage. If only they knew what Mut had just done! More villagers pressed in, surrounding her, and she found herself gasping for freedom. She looked for a way out. Knowing she could squeeze through the tiniest of spaces, she darted between two men and set off.

'Hey! Where are you going?' called the villagers.

There were people ahead, up the street. People in the doorways of their houses. People shouting out behind her, telling her to come back. Isis looked around wildly and saw a little alleyway. Impulsively, she dashed down it and up some steps on to the roof of a house, then ran along the flat rooftops, jumping nimbly from one to another. The houses were built side by side, and the rooftop walls were not high – but she guessed that not many could follow.

None did. From her rooftop vantage point, Isis surveyed the view. The main street ran roughly from north to south, and the mountain with its cemetery stretched high in front of her. Plumes of smoke rose from the houses' open courtyards, and Isis caught glimpses of women tending ovens, and servants grinding grain.

She was on the roof of a tiny house. She peeped down into the courtyard and saw a figure pacing up and down. Even from above, she seemed somehow familiar: a girl about the same age as Isis, with a slender frame much like her own. Isis listened, and heard a muffled sob. She crept closer, and saw that one arm was bandaged. There was no doubt about it – the girl in the courtyard was Tiya.

Isis wiped her own tears away. She stood at the top of the steps and waited for a minute or two, checking that Tiya was on her own. But there was no sign of anyone else, and no sound other than Tiya's weeping.

Quietly, she descended, one step at a time. Tiya had stopped pacing, and had slumped down miserably in the shade, hugging her knees and rocking to and fro.

Halfway down, Isis stopped. 'Tiya!' she called softly.

The girl went rigid. 'Who's there?'

Isis slipped down the last few steps. 'It's Isis. We met at the party. I'm one of the dancers from Waset.'

Tiya relaxed in relief. 'I remember.' She sniffed, and wiped her nose with her bandaged arm. 'What were you doing on our roof?'

'I'm sorry, Tiya, I didn't mean to frighten you.' Isis sat down next to her on the papyrus reed mats. 'I was trying to find my brother Hopi. He's in Rahotep's house with Seti. But they wouldn't let me in. There were guards outside and so many people, all crowding around – I couldn't bear it. I ran away.'

At the mention of her brother, Tiya went still. 'Is there news of Seti?' she whispered.

Isis shook her head. 'Not that I know. All I've heard is that he is with Rahotep. The foremen are there with him, too.'

'The foremen?' asked Tiya, her eyes dilated with fear. 'Baki and Nakht?'

'I think so,' said Isis. 'It was their guards outside . . . but I don't really know.'

Tiya's chest was heaving, her breathing rapid and shallow. She seemed close to panic. Isis thought of the gold bracelet, and was hardly surprised. But she felt sorry for Tiya, too. Like Heria, she found it hard to believe that she was guilty.

Isis twiddled her fingers, wondering what to say. Maybe it would be best to change the subject. 'That must be where you fell,' she observed, nodding at the courtyard steps.

Tiya looked at her sharply. 'Where I? No –' She stopped. 'I mean, yes,' she said, turning her face away.

Isis looked at the steps, frowning. They were well made – not even very steep, and Tiya was light and nimble like herself. 'But how?' she asked. 'Did you trip?'

'I . . . think so.'

'You *think* so? Don't you remember?' Isis was incredulous now.

Tiya bowed her head. 'Please don't ask about it,' she said. She picked nervously at the linen bandage that was wrapped around her arm. In daylight, Isis could see the splints of wood that held the bones still, poking out of the bandages. The doctor of Set Maat had done a good job.

Eventually, Tiya spoke. 'It's no use,' she said. 'If the foremen have got involved, we must be doomed. I might as well tell you the truth. I didn't fall down the steps at all.'

That was no great surprise. 'So what *did* happen?' asked Isis.

Tiya bit her lip. 'I was helping Seti,' she began, and then she spilled out her story.

As the foremen crowded in closer, Seti's body seemed to quake in fear. 'I am not lying,' he insisted. 'By the goddess who has taken my sight, I am telling you the truth. It was all my fault. I made Tiya go into the tunnel –'

'The tunnel? What tunnel?' Nakht pounced on the word.

'I found it – a tunnel leading into the mountain –'

'Found it? You mean you *made* it,' Baki cut in. 'You and who else? You did not carve it alone.'

Nakht waved a hand at Baki. 'Let him speak,' he said.

Seti shook his head. 'All I did was find it, I swear. I'm just a painter – I know nothing about digging tunnels.'

'Then you should,' commented Khonsu dryly. 'All our men know something of each other's work. But that is beside the point. Where did this tunnel lead to?'

Hopi was listening intently. Would Seti's story match with what they had found? The young painter groped over his bandages again, then let his hand fall.

'I don't know.' Seti's voice was faint. 'It was

narrow, half-blocked, full of crumbling rocks . . . I couldn't get far. So I fetched Tiya. She didn't want to come, but I insisted. She is small, and much nimbler. I wanted to see if she could get further inside. But then . . . but then . . .' Seti stopped. His shoulders were shaking.

'Go on,' Nakht pressed him.

'A section collapsed when she was clambering through. That is how her arm was broken.'

Silence fell. Hopi's mind was racing. Could it be true? He thought over what he had seen – the secret tunnel, the royal tomb. None of that fitted with what Seti described. But then he remembered something else. In the last dying light from the acacia twigs, he had seen a second dark hole in the walls of the tomb. A second hole – perhaps, indeed, a second tunnel.

'Lies,' growled Baki. 'All lies.'

'I am not so sure,' said Rahotep. 'We all know Seti. I myself have worked with him in the tombs. Is this story so unlikely? He is already suffering the wrath of the gods. I do not think he would want to anger them further.'

Baki snorted. 'He admits he has entered a tunnel. He wants us to believe that he has not entered a tomb! Brother Rahotep, you are being either stupid or naive. All we need to know now is who else is involved.'

'And what about Tiya?' queried Khonsu.

Baki shrugged. 'I heard she had fallen down some steps.'

Nakht got to his feet. 'There is only one way to find out,' he said. 'We must go and question her. We will soon find out if their stories match.'

Hopi watched them go. Seti's story could be true. He *wanted* it to be true, and hoped with all his heart that Tiya's words would confirm it.

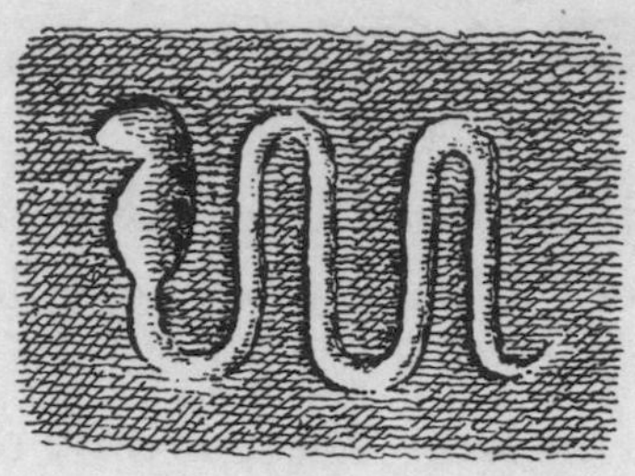

CHAPTER EIGHT

Tiya was trembling. Isis stood close by her side as she faced the most important men in the village.

'Tell us how you broke your arm,' said Nakht.

'I fell,' whispered Tiya. She nodded towards the courtyard steps. 'Down there.'

Isis felt alarmed. She had heard the story from beginning to end, but now Tiya was backtracking! It seemed very foolish.

Baki turned to the others in satisfaction. 'You see? Seti must be lying.'

'Seti . . .' Tiya's voice was anguished. 'What's happened to him?'

'He will live. But he will no longer see,' Khonsu told her.

Tiya let out a little sob. She swayed, and Isis feared

she would fall. She placed an arm around her while the men waited for her to recover.

Then Nakht spoke. 'Your brother has told us something different,' he said. 'Are you still going to stick to this story?'

'Tell them the truth, Tiya,' Isis whispered.

Tiya was silent. Then she sighed heavily, as though defeated, and stepped towards a wooden box in the corner of the room. Isis caught a glimpse of soft linen and beaded jewellery as Tiya rummaged in its depths. She plucked something out and walked over to the men, her arm outstretched. On the palm of her hand lay the gold bracelet.

'Is this what you are looking for?' she asked.

Isis guessed it wasn't. The three men gaped, their eyes bulging. Isis saw a smile curl at the corner of Baki's mouth, which he quickly wiped away.

'What did I say?' exclaimed Baki. 'This is all the evidence we need.'

'Take it,' whispered Tiya. 'Take it away. It is cursed. We thought it was a blessing from the gods, but it has brought us nothing but pain.'

'How could you be blessed by something you had stolen?' queried Khonsu.

Tiya's eyes flew open in protest. 'It isn't stolen!'

'My dear, this is a royal bracelet,' said Nakht. 'It

cannot possibly be yours.'

'But . . . but what if something is found?' Tiya's eyes searched those of the foremen.

'Well, that depends,' said Nakht. 'Explain yourself.'

'Seti found it. He took it as a gift from the goddess, for that part of the mountain belongs to no one but her.'

'And where is that?' enquired Khonsu.

'High up, towards the Great Place,' replied Tiya. She hesitated. 'Near the entrance to a tunnel.'

'Don't you mean a tomb?' asked Baki.

'No. Just a crumbling tunnel. Seti took me up there to see if I could crawl in further, but the rocks shifted. One of them fell and landed on my arm. That is how it was broken.'

Baki snorted. 'You possess a royal bracelet, but you haven't seen a tomb?'

Tiya shook her head vehemently. 'No, no. We never saw a tomb.'

The three men were silent. Nakht took the bracelet from Tiya and studied it, a deep frown on his face.

'So. Their stories match,' said Khonsu, eventually.

'Yes.' Nakht nodded agreement.

But Baki placed a hand on Nakht's shoulder. 'Brother, brother,' he murmured, 'of course their stories match. They must have made them up long ago. Meretseger herself has brought Seti to our attention, and his sister has shown us this bracelet. What further proof do you need?'

His words had a deep effect on Tiya. She sank to her knees and began to sob. 'Please believe me,' she wept. 'I have told you everything. I swear I have told you the truth.'

Nakht and Khonsu looked troubled. 'We have no choice, brothers,' said Khonsu. 'Baki is right. The evidence does go against her.'

'I am glad you see sense at last,' said Baki. 'We must call the guards and place her under arrest.'

Hopi hurried out on to the street. He had been in the house of Rahotep much, much longer than he'd intended, and he limped as fast as he could to Heria's house. The front door was ajar, and he pushed it open, hoping to hear the chatter of girls' voices. The house was silent.

His heart sank. Much as he was interested in the village events, it was his family that mattered most. Surely they wouldn't have left him . . .

'Is anyone there?' he called.

Still nothing. Hopi made his way through the house cautiously, looking into each of the rooms as he passed. They were all empty. Then he heard something. A noise in the courtyard; perhaps a scuffling of feet. Then silence again.

He crept to the threshold. There, a strange sight met his eyes. Mut sat in a corner, with her young brothers Ramose and Kha cuddled up close to her. All three seemed frozen in fear, and were staring at something beside the bread oven.

Mut pointed. She seemed unable to speak.

Hopi stepped forward and peered around the oven, his heart beating faster. What he saw was very familiar, with a yellow body and fat, upturned tail.

'A scorpion,' he said. 'Is that all?'

A tiny sound squeaked from Mut's mouth.

Hopi turned to look at her. Mut's eyes were dilated with terror and her little brothers clung to her, hiding their faces. His smile faded. Somehow, he had never taken her fear seriously before. He had thought she'd been making a fuss over nothing. But there was no doubting it now.

'Don't worry, I won't let it hurt you,' he said.

Hopi looked around. He wouldn't say so to Mut, but this fat-tailed scorpion was particularly dangerous. Its sting could be fatal; it would be foolish to try handling it. Instead, he reached for one of the pottery bowls that lay stacked against the courtyard wall. In one deft movement, he clapped it upside down over the scorpion, trapping it underneath.

'There,' he said. 'You're perfectly safe.'

'Take it away,' Mut whispered.

Hopi looked around for something flat. There was a wooden tray in one corner, which he picked up and slid under the bowl. Now the scorpion was in a little cage. 'I'll take it up to the cemetery,' he said. 'I won't be long.'

Mut nodded dumbly. Hopi lifted the makeshift cage and headed out on to the street. Curious faces watched him and whispers followed him as he trod the now-familiar route to the cemetery gate. He ignored them all, concentrating on not letting the pottery bowl slip.

By a mound of boulders, Hopi put down the tray and took off the bowl. The scorpion was still for a moment, then shot off, disappearing between the rocks. Hopi smiled. It was always good to give a creature its freedom. He glanced up at the mountain and was surprised to see several figures high on the cliff path. He shaded his eyes. One of them looked oddly familiar. Paneb . . . and, by his side, the chubby form of Heria.

Paneb and Heria? What were they doing up there? Suddenly, Hopi realised that things weren't right.

Why had the boys been left alone with Mut? Where was the rest of the family? And most importantly, where was Isis?

He rushed back to Heria's house. Ramose and Kha ran up to him and hugged his legs as Mut came to the door to greet him.

'You saved us!' laughed Ramose.

'Yes. Thank you,' said Mut. She looked at him shyly, and smiled.

Hopi couldn't remember Mut ever thanking him for anything. 'That's all right,' he said. 'I like scorpions. But where is everyone? Where's Isis?'

Mut's smile vanished. She turned her back, bowing her head. 'I don't know,' she muttered.

Hopi's heart plummeted. So something *was* wrong. 'What do you mean, you don't know?' he asked. 'I left her here with Heria. They were going to wait for me to get back.'

'We had a fight,' mumbled Mut. 'She ran away. Heria tried to follow, but Isis is quick . . . she soon lost her. Some people saw her run off over the rooftops, so everyone thinks she's gone up on to the mountain, like last time. Mother and Father and the others are looking for her. That's why I'm here with the boys.'

So that was it. Hopi went cold. 'I'll find her,' he

said mechanically, turning towards the door. 'I have to find her.'

'I'm sorry, Hopi,' said Mut. 'It was my fault.'

Isis was frightened. The foremen had taken Tiya away to be guarded in Nakht's house. It wouldn't be long before they arrested Seti, too. She looked around, wondering who else lived in the little house. To her surprise, she found an elderly woman dozing in the front room. She opened her eyes as Isis entered, but only stared ahead, mumbling.

'Hello,' whispered Isis, taking her hand. 'Are you Tiya's mother?'

A smile creased the old woman's face. 'Mother of her mother,' she managed to say. 'Where is Tiya? It's time for my bread.'

Isis was horrified. How could she tell this old woman that her granddaughter had been arrested? And who else was there to look after her? There didn't seem to be anyone other than Seti. With a sudden flood of conviction, Isis felt sure that Tiya was innocent. She and Hopi had seen a different tunnel, a tunnel that was still in use. They had to tell someone about it – before it was too late.

'Tiya isn't here. But she will come back,' she promised the old woman. 'I'll fetch you some bread.'

Isis ran into the courtyard. She found a little pile of flat loaves stacked by the side of the oven, and picked a couple of them up. The old woman accepted them with a smile, and mumbled thanks.

Now there was no time to waste. Isis bounded up the courtyard steps and back on to the roof. She glanced down at the street below. It was alive with gossip – many had seen Tiya being taken away, and the rest had soon heard about it. 'Shocking,' she heard. 'Dreadful.' 'Our neighbour, too.' She pulled back from the edge. She couldn't go down there.

But she had to find Hopi. She had to talk it through with him, and decide who to tell. But where would he be now? Would he still be in the house of Rahotep, or would he have left? He'd had plenty of time to say goodbye.

There wasn't much choice. Isis was not going back to Heria's house. Rahotep's house was worth a try. She looked around, trying to remember which way she'd come. Then she set off, leaping lightly over the low walls that ran around each rooftop.

Out on the street, Hopi stared up at the mountain beyond the cemetery. Why ever were they looking for Isis up there? She had no reason to head out of the village. Hopi knew that she would be doing only one thing: she'd be looking for him.

'Rahotep's house,' he muttered to himself. 'She'll show up there eventually.'

He limped back up the street to the last house in the row, and knocked. But before anyone could answer, he heard a voice.

'Psst! Hopi!'

He looked round. Rahotep's next-door neighbour stood in her doorway holding a broom, keeping an eye on developments.

'Hopi! Up here!'

He looked up. There was Isis, peeping down from the roof. He felt a wave of relief. 'Isis!' he exclaimed. 'The whole family's looking for you up on the mountain!'

'I don't care!' cried Isis. 'They can look for me all they like! Listen, Hopi. Tiya has been arrested. I saw everything. I need to talk to you.'

Hopi gazed up at his sister. How typical of Isis, to say she didn't care. But as her news sunk in, he realised that Rahotep's door still hadn't opened. Perhaps Tiya's arrest had something to do with it.

'Go down into the courtyard,' he called up to her. 'Tell Rahotep to let me in.'

Isis nodded and disappeared.

A few minutes later, Rahotep's servant opened the

door a tiny crack. When he saw Hopi, he opened it a fraction wider. Hopi squeezed inside. Then the servant banged the door shut, and barred it. Hopi walked through to the courtyard and found Seti sitting in the shade with his back against the courtyard wall, his eyes still bandaged.

Isis was explaining herself to Rahotep, but now she rushed up to Hopi and gave him a hug. 'I'm so glad I've found you!'

'*I'm* glad I've found *you*,' said Hopi. 'We've got to go, Isis. I saw Paneb and Heria right up on the mountain. We must let everyone know that you're safe.'

Isis shook her head stubbornly. 'Not after what Mut said,' she objected. 'Anyway, we have to do something, Hopi. We can't leave until we've told someone what we know.' She looked at him meaningfully.

'But –' Hopi still wasn't sure.

'We *have* to,' insisted Isis. 'I don't believe Tiya is guilty. Or Seti. Do you?'

Hopi shook his head. 'Well, no, but . . .' He was fretting. They were in enough trouble, and he didn't like to think of Nefert's wrath when she found out that Isis had been in the village all along.

'Hopi!' Isis lowered her voice. 'Look at Seti. We have to help him. And we don't have much time.'

Hopi glanced at the figure sitting against the wall.

He was a pitiful sight, the visible parts of his face still ugly and swollen. Isis was right. The family would just have to wait.

'In that case, I think this is the man we must tell.' And he turned towards the priest of Serqet.

Rahotep looked from one to the other. 'And what do you have to tell me?' he asked quietly.

Hopi took a deep breath. He might as well plunge straight in. 'There is a secret tunnel through the mountainside. It leads to a royal tomb. It is small but well built, with no crumbling rocks, so it is not the one that Seti described. But inside the tomb, there are two holes. It is possible that there is a second tunnel – a tunnel that collapsed.'

Rahotep looked startled. 'And how do you know this?'

Isis and Hopi answered together. 'We've seen it,' they said.

'Of course, Seti could have helped to build either tunnel,' Hopi carried on. 'But I don't think he did, because I overheard one of the robbers on the mountain path early yesterday morning.'

Rahotep narrowed his eyes. 'A robber? How do you know?'

'He was with a young boy – too young to be an apprentice. The boy was terrified of the wrath of the goddess. And the man said something that didn't make sense at the time. I remember it perfectly.' Hopi thought for a second, to make sure he got the wording right. '"The first one was badly made and in the wrong place." That's what he said.'

The priest of Serqet folded his arms. 'And you think he was referring to the tunnel found by Seti. And the second, one assumes, is the one found by you.'

'That's right,' said Hopi.

'Remarkable,' murmured the priest. 'And who is this man? Did you recognise him?'

'Not at first,' said Hopi. 'I only realised who he was this morning. We went into his house and I saw the young boy as well.' He hesitated. 'He is a powerful man, that is the problem.'

'Powerful or not, we must know who he is.'

Hopi nodded. 'He is one of your foremen. Baki.'

Silence fell. Isis felt heavy with fear. If one of the most powerful villagers was behind the robbery, how could they ever bring him to justice?

'We are doomed.' Seti buried his bandaged head in his hands. 'There is no hope. He will make sure that Tiya and I are found guilty. We are condemned, we will be sentenced to death.'

'Hush, Seti.' The priest of Serqet marched to and fro, his brow furrowed in thought. Then, suddenly, he stopped. 'We must not forget the power of the goddess!' he exclaimed. Snapping his fingers for his servant, Rahotep reached for a flagon of water. 'Fetch me clean linen cloths,' he said, 'and a shallow bowl.'

'Yes, sir.' The servant hurried to do as he said.

Rahotep poured water into the bowl, then crouched down in front of Seti. Carefully, he unwrapped the linen bandages. Then he dipped a soft cloth into the water, and wiped away the ointment that covered Seti's eyes. The flesh around them was still red and puffy, and he dabbed gently so as not to cause pain. Hopi and Isis drew closer, watching him work.

When he had finished, Rahotep cupped Seti's face in his hands, and stared at him intently. 'Seti,' he said, 'open your eyes.'

It seemed almost impossible, but Isis saw a flicker, and the tiniest slits appeared.

'What do you see?' demanded Rahotep.

'It . . . it's all blurred.'

Rahotep reached down for the cloth, rinsed it out and wiped Seti's eyes again.

'Now,' he said. 'Try again.'

This time, the slits were slightly wider. 'I . . .' Seti

stopped. He lifted one of his hands, and waved it slowly in front of his face. He peered at it, bringing it closer, then taking it further away. He frowned, as though he couldn't quite believe what had happened. His mouth quivered, then broke into a broad smile. 'I can see.' He gave a peal of laughter, and leaped to his feet. 'I can *see*!'

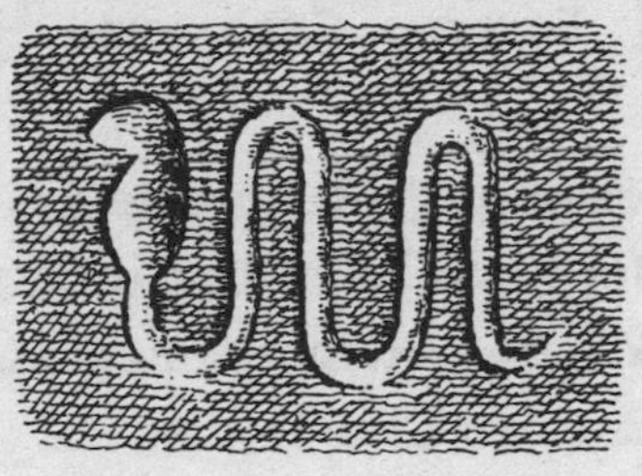

CHAPTER NINE

Seti began to run around the courtyard, calling out the names of everything he saw. 'It's a water flagon! A bread oven! A string of onions! Look, look – it's a beautiful statue!' he cried, and reached out to touch the scorpion on top of the statue of Serqet. Rahotep smiled, but then lapsed back into his thoughts.

A strange realisation dawned on Hopi. For the first time in his life, he had actually helped someone to recover from the attack of a dangerous snake. Rahotep had said so, hadn't he? *I have done all I can. But you did more.*

'It's a miracle!' shouted Seti. He turned to Hopi and flung an arm around him. 'Hopi! The goddess has forgiven me, after all!'

Rahotep came out of his reverie. 'You have

received the blessing of the goddess Serqet,' he said quietly. 'And Hopi has been her instrument of healing. But come. We must take the next step, and gather witnesses. There is no time to lose.'

The priest of Serqet took Seti by the arm and guided him out of the courtyard towards the street. He seemed calm, decisive, as though he knew exactly what to do. Hopi felt stirrings of hope. Perhaps Rahotep would know how to get the better of Baki, after all.

As soon as they were outside, Rahotep began to call out, 'Neighbours! Friends! Come out of your houses! Come forth, all those who saw the work of Meretseger this morning!'

He didn't need to wait long. The day's events had kept the villagers out on the street gossiping all day. The narrow street began to fill up. In seconds, a crowd had gathered, pushing and jostling towards the priest. Rahotep held up a hand for silence, and drew Seti to his side, placing his other hand on the young painter's shoulder.

'Who can say that this man was blinded?' he asked.

A chorus of voices answered.

'I saw it! I saw him in the cemetery!' called one woman.

'I saw him being carried to your house!' shouted another.

'And I helped to carry him down the mountain,' added a boy.

'Will you swear to it?' asked Rahotep.

'Of course!' cried the crowd.

Rahotep raised his hand again. 'Neighbours, you are our witnesses,' he said, in a solemn voice. 'This morning, you all saw that Seti was blind. But the goddess has not condemned him. Now he can see!' He turned to face Seti and raised his arms high to the heavens. 'Seti, what am I doing?'

Seti rubbed his eyes. 'You're putting your arms above your head.'

A murmur rippled through the crowd.

'He can see. He can see. A miracle! He is blessed! The goddess has lifted her curse!'

'Meretseger! Let us praise Meretseger! Let us take thanks to her shrine!'

But then Hopi became aware of a commotion at the back of the crowd. The villagers went quiet, and began to part to make way for three men. Hopi's heart sank. It was Baki, Nakht and Khonsu. They had come looking for Seti.

Silence fell as the three men stood before Rahotep.

'Brother, you know why we have come,' said Nakht. His voice was sorrowful, as though he were carrying out his duty with great regret.

'I do,' said Rahotep. 'I was indeed expecting you. But things are not as they seem, my brothers.'

Baki clucked his tongue impatiently. 'We do not have time to listen to your theories, Rahotep,' he said. 'We are here to arrest Seti, as you know very well.'

The priest of Serqet did not respond. Instead, he turned to Seti and raised his hand. 'Tell me,' he said in a soft voice. 'How many fingers am I holding up?'

Seti's face was slowly looking more normal and now his eyes were quite visible under their swollen lids. 'I can see three,' he said.

Rahotep nodded. 'Thank you,' he said. He turned to the three men. 'You see, Seti has recovered his sight. The goddess has sent a message, but it may not be the one we thought it was. We need to dig deeper, my brothers.'

Baki scowled. 'If he can see, so much the better. He will be better equipped to face the accusations against him,' he snapped. 'We have spoken to his sister Tiya. She, too, is under arrest. You can't protect him from his fate, Rahotep.'

A faint smile appeared on Rahotep's face. Hopi saw that he was ready for this. The priest turned to the crowd. 'You are my witnesses,' said the priest of Serqet. 'Has a miracle occurred among us today?'

The villagers looked at each other. Hopi saw that they were afraid of defying the foremen.

But then one woman nodded. 'Yes,' she said, 'I saw Seti blinded. And now he can see.'

'Yes, yes,' murmured others around her. 'We cannot deny it.'

Now Rahotep drew himself up to his full height, and began to speak. 'We all know that the gods are displeased with our village,' he said. 'But the gods have sent some very unusual tools.'

The three men looked puzzled. 'Tools?' asked Khonsu.

Rahotep indicated Isis and Hopi. 'Our visitors,' he said. 'They are our tools. Hopi has already played a role in Seti's healing. Now it is time for he and his sister to play another. They are young. They know little of the life of our village. Would you agree?'

'Well, yes, absolutely,' said Nakht. 'But I don't see –'

'For that reason,' Rahotep continued, 'we can be sure that they are innocent and untainted by the evil in our midst.' He looked Baki in the eye. 'They have seen things with fresh eyes, and brought remarkable things to my attention.'

'So what do you want them to do?' growled Baki.

'I ask that they be allowed to enter and search your house, Foreman Baki.'

Isis felt stunned. And scared. Foreman Baki was glaring directly at her with smouldering wrath in his eyes.

'How dare you!' the foreman roared. 'Rahotep, you overstep the line!'

'I am aware of that,' said Rahotep calmly. 'That is precisely why I have asked you before witnesses. But, my brother Baki, surely you can have no objection. These two are mere children, due to leave our village today. If there is nothing to find, they will not find it.'

Baki's big, square face seemed to explode with rage. He turned to Nakht and Khonsu. 'Brothers, you stand there and say nothing! This is an outrage! A minor priest challenging our authority – such a thing cannot be allowed!'

But Nakht and Khonsu exchanged glances. Nakht looked deeply uncomfortable. 'My brother . . .' He hesitated, looking around at the sea of eager faces. 'This is very difficult. These children can do no harm, and Rahotep would demand nothing without good reason. If you refuse, the people will not be satisfied, and tongues will never stop wagging.'

A murmur of agreement ran through the crowd. 'Yes! Let the visitors enter!' shouted a woman from the back.

Isis saw that every villager was agog with curiosity, and guessed that no one had ever dared to challenge the authority of the foremen before. The excitement was tangible, and infectious.

Baki began to protest all over again, but now the crowd was taking matters into its own hands. There was a surge along the street as everyone turned towards the foreman's house.

A woman reached out and clasped Isis's hand. 'Come, come!' she cried. 'We will show you the way!'

Isis grabbed Hopi in turn, and let herself be carried along by the tide of people milling and jostling towards Baki's house. Then she felt herself being pushed to the front. She and Hopi stood before the house that they had entered that morning, looking up into the face of the guard.

'Open the door!' cried the crowd. 'Baki's servants and womenfolk must come out! The visitors must be allowed in!'

The guard looked flustered. 'On whose authority?' he demanded.

A chorus of voices answered him: 'Foreman Nakht! Khonsu the scribe! The priest of Serqet!'

The guard searched the crowd for confirmation. Isis saw Nakht give a little nod. She stood close to Hopi as the guard brought out Baki's wife, young daughters and servants. Then she and her brother stepped in. The door closed behind them, and they stood together on the threshold of Baki's front room, with the sound of the crowd muffled on the street behind them.

They stared around the dim mud-brick house with its small but exquisitely decorated rooms. Shafts of light shone in from the courtyard at the back, giving a bluish tinge to the whitewash.

'Where should we start?' whispered Isis.

Hopi peered into the front room, which was painted with images of the household gods Bes and Tawaret. There was an altar in one corner and a birthing bed in another, but there were no nooks and crannies that might contain treasure.

'Let's take a look at the stores,' said Hopi. 'And the back rooms. Baki won't have hidden anything where visitors might see.'

Isis nodded. She tiptoed forward. 'It's creepy, searching somebody else's house,' she muttered.

Hopi knew what she meant. He felt as though they were trespassing. They passed the entrance to a storeroom and he ducked his head to check inside. It was gloomy, but as his eyes adjusted he saw sacks of grain, bags of dried beans and lentils, flagons of wine, a string of onions and some garlic, a couple of pots of honey . . . but nothing else. He stepped right inside and felt around the walls.

'Can you see anything?' enquired Isis, behind him.

Hopi pulled out of the storeroom, shaking his head. 'Nothing. Let's carry on.'

They checked the middle room of the house, and then the back room, which had another storeroom leading off it. Each of the main rooms had fine furnishings – wooden beds with elegant headrests, chairs with pretty inlays and statues of both wood and stone. There were caskets, too, containing linen garments, fine oils and perfumes, wigs and jewellery. But although there were some lovely pieces, there was nothing that looked as though it belonged in a royal tomb.

They searched the courtyard, which was half open to the sky, with just a rough palm-frond roof sheltering one side of it. It contained nothing but firewood, a grain-grinder, a bread oven and cooking implements.

'I'll just run up and check the roof,' Isis said, and

she skipped nimbly up the courtyard steps. She was soon back, shaking her head. 'Nothing but mats,' she reported.

Hopi was beginning to feel panicky. It was because of him that Baki had been accused. If they didn't find anything, the foreman's revenge might be terrible. He took a few deep breaths.

'Isis, we have to think,' he said. 'If you were Baki, where would you hide royal treasure?'

Isis frowned. 'I don't think I'd hide it in my own home at all,' she said.

Hopi swallowed. His sister's words made sense. 'No,' he agreed, 'I'd smuggle it out and sell it as fast as I could.'

So even if Baki was guilty, they couldn't prove a thing. What had Rahotep been thinking of, getting them to enter his house like this? Now they were in real trouble – and so were Seti and Tiya.

The crowd outside was getting noisier, impatient with waiting. 'Hurry up! Come out! Tell us what you have found!' came the muffled cry.

Isis and Hopi stared at each other. Hopi's mouth felt dry.

'We just have to tell them the truth,' said Isis. 'It's not our fault, Hopi.'

'No, but . . .' Hopi trailed off, his mind drifting to

Baki's furious stare. He shrugged. 'I suppose you're right.'

They started back towards the door, their hearts quaking. Hopi stared at the walls, the ceiling, the floor, hoping for a last-minute revelation. But they were all solid mud-brick, thick and impenetrable.

They passed the first storeroom. Suddenly, Isis stopped. 'Hopi,' she said, 'if you were going to smuggle treasure out of the village, how would you do it?'

Hopi frowned. 'What do you mean, how?'

Isis looked towards the storeroom, with its sacks stuffed full of grain. He saw what she was getting at.

'Yes!' he cried.

Together, they squeezed inside the store and plunged their hands into two of the bulging sacks. Hopi felt the smooth emmer wheat slip between his fingers and dug deeper, pushing and groping.

'I can feel something!' exclaimed Isis, her voice breathless.

At the same time, Hopi's fingers curled around something smooth and hard. 'So can I.'

With a little more effort, they both teased the items free from the shifting grain and lifted them out. Even in the dim light, the glint of gold made them gasp. Hopi held a wine goblet of cedar and beaten gold, while Isis held a statuette of the god Anubis, a miniature jackal formed of the blackest ebony, sitting on a golden plinth with the details of his features also picked out in gold.

They gazed at the objects open-mouthed for several seconds.

'I've never seen anything so beautiful,' murmured Isis.

Hopi felt a rush of excitement. 'There must be more!'

They balanced the objects on top of the sacks of pulses and delved into the grain again. Hopi fished out a bundle of gold pieces, which looked as though they had been stripped from chariots or furniture, while Isis found a casket containing alabaster jars of precious ointments.

A loud banging on the door interrupted their search.

'We've found enough,' said Hopi. 'All we need to do is bring Nakht and Rahotep to see the sacks. And Khonsu, of course.'

Isis held up a jewel-studded ceremonial dagger, gazing at it wistfully. 'I suppose so,' she said. 'We'll probably never see treasure like this again in our whole lives.'

They climbed out of the storeroom just as the crowd lost patience. The door burst open, and guards marched in with Nakht and Baki behind them. Rahotep and Khonsu followed. Isis and Hopi faced them, the dagger and golden goblet in their hands.

Baki gave a high-pitched roar of rage and leaped forward. Before he could even think of trying to dodge, Hopi found himself on the ground, choking, with the foreman's strong, gnarled hands around his throat.

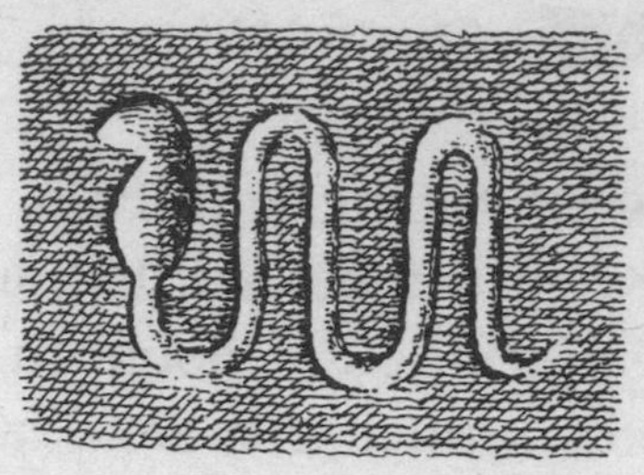

CHAPTER TEN

Isis screamed in terror. Without thinking, she raised the ceremonial dagger above her head and brought it crashing down on Baki's right arm. The blade, made for a king's tomb rather than war, was blunt – but not too blunt. The foreman gave a howl of pain as blood welled up and ran down his arm. He let go of Hopi while Nakht and Rahotep joined the guard in pulling Baki to his feet.

'Brother, brother,' remonstrated Nakht, his face tight with shock, 'control yourself. These are mere children –'

'Children!' The word burst from Baki like a thunderclap. Flecks of spittle sat upon his lips, and his nostrils flared wide. He looked wildly around him, as though he might find an escape from his situation, but he was surrounded. There was no way out.

Nakht bowed his head. 'I have known you for so many years, my brother,' he said, his voice broken with regret. 'I believed in you as a fellow servant of our king. This,' he waved a hand at the goblet and the blood-stained dagger, 'this I find hard to believe. And yet I must.'

Baki spat on the ground as more villagers pushed their way into the house, gasping at the sight of the treasure. 'Some use you are,' Baki growled at his guard.

The guard looked helpless. He stood with his arms hanging by his sides as more and more people jostled their way in.

Nakht turned to a teenage boy. 'Go and fetch the head of our Medjay,' he told him. 'Quickly.' Then he turned to the rest of the villagers. 'You must leave,' he ordered. 'You have been valuable witnesses. But it is time to restore order to our village. We must appease the gods – especially the goddess Ma'at, who is our arbiter of justice.'

Reluctantly, the people began to file back into the street. Isis watched them go with the dagger still dangling from her fingers. Then she realised that the traffic was not one way. Other people were still pushing forward, trying to get into the house.

Something was going on.

'Yes, yes, they're in there!' she heard someone say.

'Then let us through!'

Isis recognised the voice. It was Paneb, elbowing his way past the villagers – and right behind him as he entered the house were Nefert, Sheri and Kia.

'Wherever –' Nefert began, then stopped.

Hopi could guess exactly what she'd been about to say: *Wherever have you been?* They'd been looking for Isis on the mountain ever since early morning, and it must now be early afternoon. Both Nefert and Paneb looked tired and cross, but their expressions changed as they took in the scene before them.

'Whatever's happening?' asked Paneb. 'Isis, Hopi, you are not in trouble, I hope?'

'Far from it,' Rahotep replied for them. 'They have been used by the gods to reveal a terrible truth to our village.'

'Indeed,' agreed Nakht. 'And there is more to come. Where did you find these items? Are there others?'

'Oh, yes,' said Isis eagerly. 'There are sackfuls of them.' And she pointed at the storeroom with its sacks of grain. 'We've already found lots of gold and beautiful jewels.'

Hopi saw that this was not good news as far as Nakht was concerned. The deeper the guilt of his friend and colleague Baki, the more he felt betrayed.

Nakht sighed. 'These will be investigated fully in due course.'

Nefert and Paneb looked stunned. They watched in wonder as the head of the village Medjay police entered and bowed his head respectfully to both Nakht and Baki.

'What –' began Nefert again, but she was silenced by Paneb.

Nakht turned to Baki. 'Brother Baki, I will not see you paraded through the village like a common criminal,' he said. He turned to the head of police. 'You will no longer take orders from Foreman Baki. He is to be placed under arrest. But in accordance with his high status, he will remain in this house with his family. You can guard him here.'

'May I suggest that Tiya be released?' added Rahotep. 'Surely you no longer consider her guilty.'

Nakht and Khonsu exchanged glances. 'She was found in possession of royal jewellery,' said Khonsu, 'so we must conduct a thorough search of her house. But her story, and that of her brother Seti, have so far been confirmed by today's events – and especially by the blessing of the goddess.'

'But one thing still puzzles me,' said Nakht.

'And what is that?' asked Rahotep.

'Tiya and Seti speak of a tunnel that had already collapsed by the time they found it. That was some weeks ago. But these treasures must have been stolen recently, for no one would risk keeping them for long. How is that possible, if the tunnel they found was blocked?'

'We can tell you that!' Isis burst out.

The priest of Serqet smiled. 'Indeed. I think you will find, Nakht, that our visitors have played an extraordinary role in unravelling this mystery. Let us confirm their story, and that of Tiya and Seti, by visiting the mountain itself.'

A long, straggling line of people began the steep climb up the path towards the Great Place. Isis gazed back at them, shading her eyes. It looked as though half the villagers were following, so excited were they about the scandal in their midst. She skipped back to the front of the line, where Rahotep, Nakht and Khonsu were leading with Seti and Tiya, Hopi and Heria just behind them. Nefert, Paneb and the rest of the family had gone to find Mut and her brothers.

The sun was beating down relentlessly. Heria was

struggling, and had to stop to wipe her forehead every few metres. Hopi's limp was growing more pronounced, while the village elders, used to walking in the cool of evening and dawn, slowed to a plod as well. They reached the top of the cliffs and paused to survey the view.

'See the wonders of our land,' said Nakht, gesturing towards the emerald green of the fields, and the magnificent mortuary temples. 'See what the gods have given us. And yet the work of Seth is never finished. However much we have to be thankful for, he still sows chaos among us.'

Khonsu placed a hand on his shoulder. 'Don't grieve so, my brother,' he said. 'Seth may do his worst, but Horus always triumphs in the end.'

They carried on until the desert stretched out on their left, unfolding into the great Sahara, and walked as far as the workmen's huts above the Great Place.

Hopi pointed to a winding gully. 'The open tunnel is that way,' he told Nakht.

'Then we shall go there first,' said the foreman.

There was no path down into the gully – just a slope of limestone pebbles and rocks. The group began their descent slowly, sometimes sliding on treacherous loose stones. Isis remembered wandering into the gully from the opposite direction, disorientated and lost, and seeing Hopi slumped ahead. Approaching the tunnel now, straight from the path, it seemed incredible that they had ever found it – in a gully of endless crags, fallen rocks and fissures, they had located the one fissure that hid something behind it.

Nakht and Khonsu examined the entrance to the tunnel closely, Nakht running his fingers over the scorings of the chisels.

'The workmanship is of our own men,' he said sadly. 'I had hoped, even now, that it might not be so.'

Khonsu turned to Seti. 'But this is not the tunnel that you discovered?'

Seti shook his head. 'No. That's in the next gully.'

The group toiled up the ridge in the afternoon heat. At the top, Seti pointed to an outcrop of rocks below. 'There,' he said.

'Very well.' Rahotep nodded.

Isis bounded ahead, leaping lightly to the bottom of the gully where the outcrop lay. She gazed up at hulking boulders, deep golden ochre against the blue sky, and clambered around them to see if she could find the entrance herself.

It didn't take long. In the shadow cast by the rocks she found a patch of deeper shade, a blackness leading into the heart of the mountain. She crouched down and peered inside, then crawled slowly forward on all fours.

'Isis! Stop!' It was Tiya's voice, urgent and scared. 'It's not safe!'

Isis looked over her shoulder to see that the group had arrived. Everyone was gathered around the narrow entrance to the tunnel, craning their necks to see inside. She stopped and looked up. Above her head, shafts of daylight revealed the unmistakable work of chisels, which continued on into the darkness. As her eyes adjusted to the blackness, she saw the angular bulk of a freshly fallen rock.

'Tell us what you can see!' called Nakht.

Isis wriggled backwards and out into the sunlight. 'It's definitely a tunnel,' she said. 'But I can see rocks blocking it, further inside.'

Seti and Tiya smiled at her, their faces alight with relief. With great dignity, Nakht stepped forward and dropped down on to his knees, then eased his head and shoulders into the tunnel. When he emerged, his face was grave.

'Then this, at least, is true. I have seen it for myself,' he said. 'Now, Seti. You must show us where you found the bracelet.'

Seti didn't hesitate. He led the group back towards the slope for a few strides to a flat rock that jutted out at ankle height. 'It was just here,' he said, 'hidden behind this rock.'

Isis could imagine what had happened. The robbers must have been able to use this tunnel, before it collapsed. Perhaps one of them had emerged under the cover of darkness, then tripped over the jutting rock, dropping part of his precious booty. He'd have hurried on, never guessing what he'd left behind.

Hopi gazed at the tunnel, then up at the slope, imagining the same thing. He was used to scanning rocks for the slightest glimpse of snakes or scorpions, and, suddenly, something caught his eye. A tiny reflective glint. He craned forward to look at it more closely, then scooped something up with his finger.

'Look,' he said.

Everyone stared. Hopi showed his finger and thumb. Between them, there was the tiniest piece of lapis lazuli, bright blue against his flesh.

Hopi smiled. 'It must have chipped off when the robber dropped the bracelet,' he said. 'I think that provides the final proof, doesn't it? Seti couldn't have taken the bracelet from the tomb. As he said, he found it right here.'

The mountainside was alive with chatter. The villagers had been given several months' worth of gossip, at least – and it wasn't over yet. They had

Baki's accomplices to unearth; there would no doubt be trials to witness, visits from the vizier and all sorts of further excitement. But for Isis and Hopi, it was time to rejoin the troupe, and go home.

'I still don't want you to go,' said Heria, puffing along at Isis's side. 'I'll miss you, Isis.'

'Can you leave the village sometimes?' asked Isis.

'Oh yes,' said Heria. 'Father has a donkey somewhere. He hires him out, but I'm sure he could get him back.'

'Well, then. Come and visit us in Waset,' said Isis. 'It's not that far, you know.'

'I will,' Heria promised. 'And – I hope everything will be all right with Mut. It was awful, seeing you run away.'

Mut. Isis took a deep breath. Of course, after everything they had seen and heard, Nefert and Paneb couldn't be angry with her any more. But Mut . . . she didn't know how she was going to sort things out with her.

They entered the village, and the crowd began to disperse. Hopi and Isis headed with Heria and Khonsu to their home, where the family was waiting with Happy the donkey tethered outside. They were joined by Rahotep and Nakht, and, of course, Seti and Tiya.

Isis felt nervous. She hadn't seen Mut since their argument. She sidled into the courtyard, trying to make herself invisible as the explanations began. Nefert and Paneb were still a little guarded, curious as to what had been going on behind their backs, but they listened attentively as Rahotep began to speak.

'This is a painful time for our village,' the priest told them. 'We have uncovered a great crime – the robbery of a royal tomb – which is terrible indeed. Yet it would have been even more terrible if two young people had been wrongly accused and convicted. I speak of Seti and Tiya.'

The priest beckoned them, and they shyly stepped forward to stand at his side. He put an arm around each of them. 'I have worked in the tombs with Seti, and Tiya has entertained us at many of our parties,' he carried on. 'This is a close community. I was sad when Tiya broke her arm – and concerned when Seti started to seek out cobras. But I was very interested to discover Hopi's remarkable gift, which he willingly used to help Seti. Unfortunately Seti did not follow Hopi's advice; the goddess showed her displeasure and Seti was blinded. But only briefly, for Hopi once more used his gift – this time to save Seti's sight.'

'But why?' asked Paneb. 'Why would your goddess do this?'

'I have thought about this,' said Rahotep. 'As you know, our gods often reveal themselves in riddles. Seti, perhaps, has been a symbol for our village. We have all been blinded, in a sense. Blinded to the evil among us. It was Isis and Hopi who discovered the open tunnel to the tomb, and they who discovered who had built it. It was their discoveries that opened our eyes . . . just as Hopi opened Seti's.'

'Well, well,' said Paneb. He gave a rueful smile. 'Our visits are not usually so eventful.'

'This one was destined to be so,' said Nakht. 'We . . .' he corrected himself, 'I planned a party in the hope that we would discover the robbers. The plan succeeded, but not in the way I expected. I must thank you, even if it is with sorrow in my heart, for Foreman Baki is my oldest friend.' He sighed heavily. 'And now you must return to Waset. I have doubled your payment for the role your troupe has played. May the gods travel with you. Farewell.'

Nefert and Paneb were clearly delighted, but tried not to show it. Nakht turned and left, his head bowed.

'You must be getting on your way,' said Rahotep.

'But before you leave, I have something to give Hopi. Khonsu, you are a scribe. Would you bring me a piece of papyrus, and one of your writing sets?'

Khonsu did as he asked, and with everyone watching, Rahotep quickly wrote a letter in the hieratic script. He allowed the ink to dry, then rolled up the papyrus and handed it to Hopi.

'It is a letter of introduction,' said Rahotep. 'Take it to Menna, on the eastern fringes of Waset. He is the greatest priest of Serqet in the town, and I know he seeks an apprentice. We are old friends, and I have written to him of your gift. He will be only too glad to accept you.'

Hopi felt as though he were walking on a cloud. For once, he barely noticed his bad leg, because his heart was bursting with happiness. As they drew closer to the River Nile, he gazed at the town of Waset eagerly. He could hardly wait to get there, and get started. An apprentice! So he had a future, after all . . . and a future that involved his favourite creatures. It was incredible.

'Well done, Hopi,' said a quiet voice at his side. It was Mut.

'Oh, thank you, Mut,' he said. 'I still can't believe it, to be honest.'

'I can. You rescued me from the scorpion. You'll make a great priest of Serqet,' she said.

'That was nothing.' Hopi grinned.

'I didn't think so.' Mut's voice was grave. 'I was terrified.'

Hopi looked at Mut, and saw that she seemed a little nervous. 'Well, it's all over now,' he said.

'Not quite,' said Mut. 'There's something else.'

Hopi raised his eyebrows. 'And what's that?'

Mut chewed a nail. 'I have to apologise to Isis.'

Isis was up ahead, leading Happy the donkey with Ramose and Kha on board. Hopi guessed she'd been avoiding Mut. 'And is that terrifying, too?'

Mut nodded.

Hopi laughed. He knew Isis inside out. The moment she heard an apology, she'd melt.

'How about I come with you?' he offered.

Mut's shoulders relaxed. 'Yes, please,' she whispered.

'Right,' said Hopi, 'let's go.'

CAST OF CHARACTERS

Chronicle Characters

Hopi The thirteen-year-old brother of Isis. Ever since surviving the bite of a crocodile in the attack that killed their parents, Hopi has had a fascination with dangerous creatures, particularly snakes and scorpions.

Isis The eleven-year-old sister of Hopi. She is a talented dancer and performs regularly with Nefert and Paneb's troupe. Her dance partner is Mut.

Mut The eleven-year-old daughter of Paneb and Nefert, and dance partner to Isis.

Paneb Husband of Nefert, father of Mut, Ramose and Kha, and the head of the household where Isis and Hopi live. He organises bookings for the dance and music troupe.

Nefert Wife of Paneb, mother of Mut, Ramose and Kha, and sister of Sheri and Kia. She plays the lute and is head of the dance and music troupe.

Sheri One of Nefert's widowed sisters, and a musician in the troupe. She has a particularly loving nature.

Kia The second of Nefert's widowed sisters, also a musician living with the troupe. She is slightly more cold and distant than Sheri, but is hardworking and practical.

Ramose Eldest son of Nefert and Paneb, aged five. Mut's brother.

Kha Younger son of Nefert and Paneb, aged two. Mut's brother.

Menna A priest of Serqet in the town of Waset. (A priest of Serqet was someone who treated snake bites and scorpion stings.)

OTHER CHARACTERS IN THIS STORY

Nakht One of the two foremen who supervise the work in the royal tombs. Each foreman has his own team of workers. Nakht is also a village elder of Set Maat.

Baki The second of the two foremen, and a village elder.

Khonsu The principal scribe for the work in the royal tombs, who makes a note of the workers' attendance and equipment. A village elder, widowed.

Seti A young painter who has just finished his apprenticeship in the royal tombs.

Rahotep The village priest of Serqet in Set Maat, who treats snake bites and the stings of scorpions. He also works as a draughtsman in the royal tombs.

Heria The twelve-year-old daughter of Khonsu.

Tiya One of the village dancers of Set Maat, and Heria's friend.

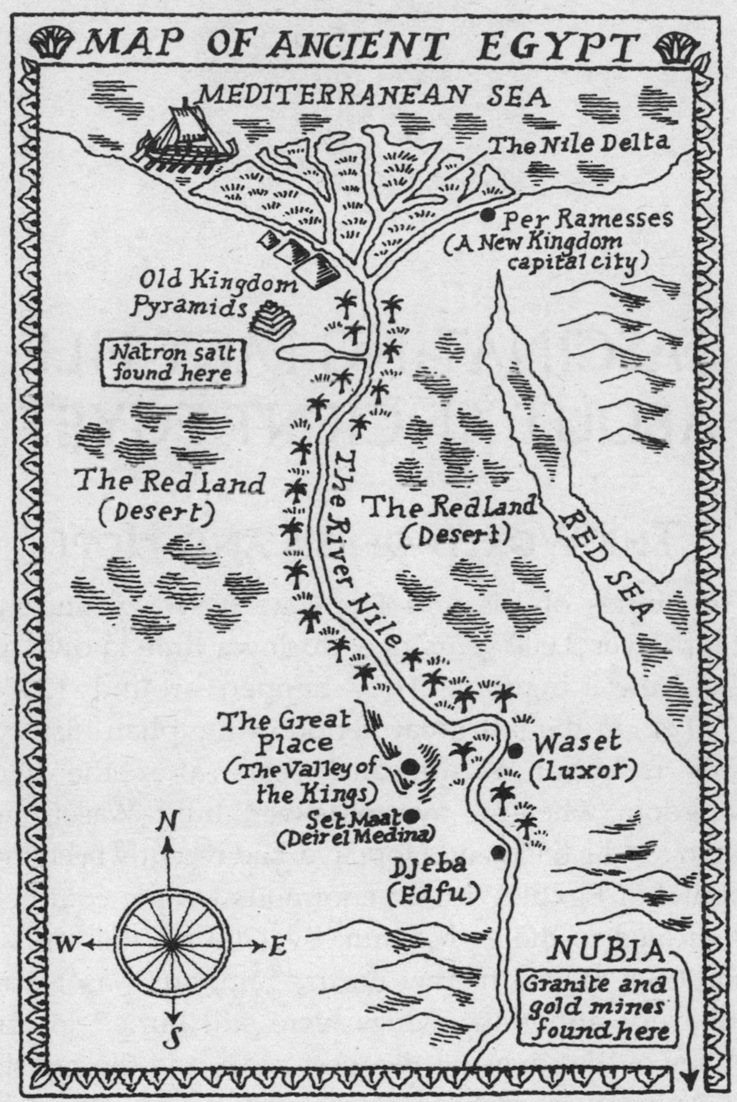
MAP OF ANCIENT EGYPT
MEDITERRANEAN SEA
The Nile Delta
Per Ramesses
(A New Kingdom
capital city)
Old Kingdom
Pyramids
Natron salt
found here
The Red land
(Desert)
The River Nile
The Redland
(Desert)
RED SEA
The Great
Place
(The Valley of
the Kings)
Set Maat
(Deir el Medina)
Waset
(Luxor)
Djeba
(Edfu)
N
S
W
E
NUBIA
Granite and
gold mines
found here

FASCINATING FACT FILE ABOUT ANCIENT EGYPT

The World of Isis and Hopi

The stories of Isis and Hopi are based in ancient Egypt over 3,000 years ago, during a time known as the New Kingdom. They happen around 1200–1150 BC, in the last great period of Egyptian history. This is about a thousand years after the Old Kingdom, when the pyramids were built. Waset, the town in which Isis and Hopi live, had recently been the capital of Egypt, with an enormous temple complex dedicated to the god Amun. By 1200 BC, the capital had been moved further north again, but Waset was still very important. Kings were still buried in the Valley of the Kings on the west bank, and the priests of Amun were rich and powerful. Today, Waset is known as Luxor; in books about ancient Egypt, it is often referred to by the Greek name of Thebes.

A LITTLE BIT ABOUT COBRAS

Cobras are easily recognised because of their habit of rearing up and spreading their 'hoods'. The cobra found by Hopi and Seti is a red spitting cobra, the only kind of spitting cobra that exists in Egypt today. The cobra's colouring varies. In Egypt it is generally olive brown, with a dark patch below the eye, but south of Egypt (in Kenya, for example), it tends to be red, which is how it got its name. When threatened, spitting cobras squirt a stream of venom at their victim's eyes. Hopi did exactly the right thing by throwing liquid into Seti's face. If the venom is not washed out, it damages the cornea and the person can go blind.

I chose this snake because of the villagers' beliefs about Meretseger. There are accounts of people pleading with the cobra goddess to restore their sight, having been struck blind. Eye complaints were common in ancient Egypt, but it occurred to me that there might have been spitting cobras around the village. In fact, though, red spitting cobras tend to live in semi-arid areas where there is some vegetation, so on the whole they would be found closer to the Nile.

As well as spitting cobras, there would have been plenty of Egyptian cobras in the area. These snakes were greatly feared. They don't spit, but they bite, and their venom is deadly.

In case you're wondering, the snake found by Hopi at the beginning of the book is a diadem snake that feeds mostly on rodents. Diadem snakes are perfectly harmless to humans. Today, some people keep them as pets.

There were a number of cobra goddesses in ancient Egypt. As well as Meretseger and Renenutet, who are both mentioned in the story, there was Wadjet, the goddess who protected Lower Egypt (the Delta area and the north). Nekhbet, a vulture goddess, protected Upper Egypt, so this is why there was always a cobra and a vulture on the crowns of Egyptian kings.

Several hieroglyphs are based on cobras. There's one of a cobra rearing up with its hood spread out, one rearing up from a basket, one wriggling along the ground, and a number of others.

SET MAAT AND THE GREAT PLACE

Set Maat (which means the 'Place of Truth') and the Great Place still exist today. The ruins of Set Maat, the tomb-builders' village, are now called Deir el Medina, while the dry desert valley that holds the kings' tombs is called the Valley of the Kings. The village was created specially as a place for the kings' craftsmen to live in while they worked on the royal tombs. Ancient Egyptian history spans about 3,000 years, but this village thrived for only 400 of them – very roughly, from 1500–1100 BC, during the New Kingdom. Before and after that, Egypt's kings lived further north and were buried there, too.

The craftsmen of Set Maat were well paid by the government, so they could afford to live well. If you look at a book about the Valley of the Kings, you can see how beautiful their work was – many of the tombs have survived, along with their amazing paintings. Some of the villagers' own tombs have also survived. They are smaller, but perhaps more interesting – while royal tombs are covered in formal paintings of the gods, the villagers' tombs have beautiful, brightly coloured paintings of the life they hoped to live in the Next World.

Probably the most famous tomb built by the villagers is the tomb of Tutankhamun. It is famous because it was discovered in 1922 with many of its treasures intact, including the king's stunning gold mask. By the time of this story, the boy king was already lying safely in his tomb. Very few Egyptian kings were lucky enough to lie undisturbed for so long.

Tomb Robberies in Ancient Egypt

You may be surprised to learn that many tombs were robbed by the ancient Egyptians themselves. Everyone knew that royalty and wealthy people were buried with lots of treasure and, as far back as the Old Kingdom, robbers found a way to steal it. In fact, the reason the Great Place existed at all was to hide the kings' tombs away from robbers. The kings thought that in this dry, desert valley, tucked away from public view, their rock-cut tombs would be safe.

They were wrong. And what's a little bit shocking is that even the villagers of Set Maat were involved in some of the robberies. There are several accounts of villagers being put on trial, accused of stealing royal goods; in one case, it seems that a group of thieves from Waset actually murdered a villager who was in on their plot.

At first, robbers targeted private tombs or the tombs of queens and lesser royals, because they were less heavily guarded. In some cases, they broke through the tomb door; in other cases, they tunnelled through the rock, as they do in this story. But it was only a matter of time before gangs of thieves set to work on the kings' tombs, too.

When the robbers got inside, the tombs were

ransacked and their contents hacked to pieces. Furniture was stripped of its gold, sarcophagi were tipped over, and mummies were ripped apart or even burned so that the thieves could take the precious amulets hidden among the wrappings.

Towards the end of the New Kingdom, the priests of Amun in Waset decided to move some of the kings' bodies, give them a new set of wrappings and hide them outside their tombs to keep them safe. So the mummies of some of Egypt's most famous kings – Seti I, Ramesses II and III, for example – were actually found jumbled together in a tomb-shaft high in the cliffs, near the mortuary temple of a famous queen called Hatshepsut. What's also probable, though, is that moving the kings was a good excuse for the priests to open up their tombs and take some of the treasure themselves.

GODS AND GODDESSES

Ancient Egyptian religion was very complicated. There wasn't just one god, but hundreds, each symbolising something different. Many of them were linked to a particular animal or plant. The Egyptians believed that their king or pharaoh was one of the gods, too.

Not everyone worshipped the same gods. It would have been very difficult to worship all of them, because there were so many. Some gods were more important than others, and some places had special gods of their own. People would have had their favourites depending on where they lived and what they did.

These are some of the most important gods of the New Kingdom, and all the special ones that are mentioned in this book.

Amun The great god of Waset (Thebes), a creator god and god of the air. When Waset became very powerful in the New Kingdom, he was combined with the sun god Re and became **Amun-Re**. He was shown with tall feathers on his head, or with a ram's head.

Anubis The god of mummies and embalming. He was usually shown with a jackal's head.

Apep The great snake god of darkness, chaos and evil. He was usually shown as an enormous serpent, but sometimes as a crocodile or even a dragon.

Bes A god who was worshipped in people's homes, rather than at shrines and temples. He was shown as a bearded dwarf, often with his tongue sticking out, and was believed to protect people's houses, pregnant women and children.

Hathor A goddess of fertility, love, music and dancing. She was usually shown as a cow, or a woman with a cow's head, or a woman with a cow's ears and horns.

Horus The falcon-headed king of the gods, who fought and won a battle with his evil uncle Seth. The reigning king of Egypt was believed to be the embodiment of Horus.

Isis The mother of Horus and wife of Osiris, the goddess of motherhood and royal protection. She was associated with the goddess Hathor.

Khepri The scarab god, the god of the rising sun. It was believed that he pushed the sun up every morning in the same way that a scarab pushes its ball of dung.

Khonsu The moon god of Waset, worshipped in the great temple complex there. He was the adopted son of Mut.

Ma'at The goddess of truth and justice, balance and order, who helped to judge people's hearts after their death.

Meretseger A cobra goddess worshipped by the villagers of Set Maat, who believed that she lived on the mountain behind the village. She was seen as a vengeful goddess who would punish the villagers if they did wrong.

Mut The great mother-goddess of Waset, worshipped with Amun and Khonsu. Because Waset is often called Thebes, these three are known as the 'Theban Triad'.

Osiris Husband of Isis, father of Horus and brother of the evil god Seth. He was the king of the underworld, so he was usually shown as a mummy.

Re (or **Ra**) The sun god, who travelled across the sky every day in a *barque* (boat).

Renenutet The cobra goddess of fertility, of nursing children and of the harvest. Farmers in particular would make offerings to her so that she would protect their crops.

Serqet The goddess of scorpions. She was believed to cure the stings and bites of all dangerous creatures like snakes and scorpions.

Seth The brother of Osiris, the god of chaos, evil and the Red Land. He was shown with the head of a strange dog-like creature that has never been identified.

Sobek The ancient Egyptian crocodile god. On the whole, he was feared by the Egyptians, but he was sometimes seen as a god of fertility, too. There were two big cult temples to Sobek – one in the north, and one south of Waset at a place that is now called Kom Ombo.

Tawaret A hippopotamus goddess who protected children and women, particularly during childbirth. Like Bes, Tawaret was worshipped in people's homes rather than in temples.

Thoth The god of writing and scribes. He was shown as an ibis, or with the head of an ibis.

GLOSSARY

acacia A small, thorny tree. Some types of acacia grow particularly well in dry, desert regions.

alabaster A whitish stone that is quite soft and easily carved. The Egyptians used it to make many beautiful objects.

amulet A lucky charm, worn to protect a person from evil.

Black Land The rich, fertile land close to the Nile, where the ancient Egyptians felt safe. They lived and grew their crops here.

carnelian A reddish stone used by the Egyptians to make jewellery.

cowrie A kind of shell used widely across Africa since ancient times. It has been found in ancient Egyptian tombs and is believed to have symbolised fertility.

emmer wheat The type of wheat that was grown in ancient Egypt. Barley was the other main food crop.

faience A sort of ceramic with a coloured glaze (often blue), used to make jewellery and amulets.

fat-tailed scorpion A very dangerous scorpion that is usually yellow with a wide tail. There is also a black variety. Its sting has been known to kill people.

flax An important Egyptian crop that provided oil (linseed oil) and cloth (linen). The ancient Egyptians made almost all their clothes from linen.

Great Place The ancient Egyptian name for what we now call the Valley of the Kings.

hieratic A shorthand version of hieroglyphics, which simplified the hieroglyphs to make them quicker to write.

hieroglyphics The ancient Egyptian system of picture writing. Each individual picture is called a **hieroglyph**.

Kingdom of the Dead Generally speaking, the west bank of the Nile was seen as the Kingdom of the Dead because the sun sets to the west.

lapis lazuli A deep blue semi-precious stone that the Egyptians valued highly. It wasn't found in Egypt, but had to be imported from modern-day Afghanistan.

limestone Along with sandstone, this was a rock commonly found in Egypt and used to build the many temples (but not houses, which were made of mud brick).

Medjay Originally a Nubian people from the south. Many Medjay joined the Egyptian army and police force, so that by the New Kingdom, the police force itself was called 'the Medjay'. The Medjay was used to guard the village of Set Maat.

mortuary temple There were two kinds of temple in ancient Egypt. Cult temples were for the worship of a particular god or gods, while mortuary temples were for the worship of a king after his death. Mortuary temples were mostly found on the west bank – the Kingdom of the Dead.

Next World The place ancient Egyptians believed they would go after death. It would be better than this world, of course, but quite similar – which was why they needed to take their bodies and many possessions with them.

Nile flood Also called 'the inundation'. Every year, the Nile river flooded, covering the fields with rich black silt. When the waters went down again, the farmers could plant their seed.

ostracon (pl. **ostraca**) A small piece of pottery or a flake of limestone used as 'scrap paper' for writing on.

papyrus A kind of reed that used to grow in the marshes alongside the Nile. It was made into many things – mats, baskets, sandals and even boats – but it is most famous for the flat sheets of 'paper' made from it, which are named after the reed.

perfume cone Pictures on the walls of tombs show women wearing rounded cones on their heads at parties. It's thought that these were made of a kind of scented fat, which would melt on to their wigs and fill the room with perfume.

pharaoh The ancient Egyptian term for their king. It was only used by the Egyptians themselves in the later stages of their history, but we now use it to refer to any ancient Egyptian king.

Red Land The desert, the land of the dangerous god Seth. It was greatly feared by the Egyptians because it was impossible to live there.

red ochre A red-coloured clay that the Egyptians ground up to make lipstick and blusher. They probably mixed it with oil or fat to put on their lips.

***sam*-plant** A plant that is mentioned in an ancient Egyptian cure for snake bites. It is hard to work out exactly which plant they meant, so we use their own name for it.

sarcophagus A big stone coffin. A smaller wooden coffin was often put inside.

scarab A kind of dung beetle that was worshipped by the Egyptians. Scarab amulets were thought to give great protection. The scarab was the creature of the god Khepri (see the Gods and Goddesses section).

spiny-tailed lizard A kind of lizard that lives in the deserts of Egypt.

Temples of a Million Years Another name for the mortuary temples on the west bank of the Nile.

tomb-chapel The little chapels that were built over a person's tomb, especially at Set Maat, where relatives could visit, pray and make offerings.

vizier The ancient Egyptian kings' second in command, who often presided over important trials.

Isis and Hopi's story continues – along the banks of the River Nile – in

THE HORNED VIPER

Read on for an exciting extract . . .

Sweat ran down the men's backs. It trickled down their foreheads and into their eyes. The ropes chafed their shoulders and hands, cutting into their flesh, so that blood mingled with the sweat.

'*Heave!*' shouted Hat-Neb, the overseer.

The men heaved, and the huge block of stone inched up the ramp.

'Useless! It's hardly moved! *Heave!*' yelled Hat-Neb. He turned to his deputy. 'What's that you've got in your hand?'

'A whip, sir.' The deputy looked troubled.

'Then why aren't you using it?' Hat-Neb's face was twisted with fury. 'These men are useless, lazy good-for-nothings. Whip them!'

The deputy looked uneasy. 'Sir, they're doing their best. Five men fell sick yesterday and cannot work.

Those that are here haven't rested since dawn.'

Hat-Neb narrowed his eyes. 'Are you disobeying me?'

The deputy said nothing. He wiped a hand across his forehead, then, reluctantly, he raised his whip and turned towards the men. The whip whistled through the air, and the men cried out in pain. The block of stone shifted a tiny bit further up the ramp.

The temple was half-built. It would be beautiful when it was finished, glistening with white paint overlaid with brilliant colours. Its images and hieroglyphs would all speak of the glory of Horus, the king of the gods.

But the building process wasn't such a beautiful sight. Things were falling behind, because a nasty sickness was spreading among the men. It made them vomit and sweat, and it left them weak and shaking. They needed to rest for several days before they could work again. But Hat-Neb was cruel and merciless. He had no sympathy. He just worked the other men harder and harder until some of them thought they would die of exhaustion.

The deputy raised his whip again, but he didn't crack it. He could see that the men were close to breaking. In fact, they were so exhausted that there was a risk they would let go of the rope altogether.

'Steady, men!' he shouted. 'Hold it there!' He turned to Hat-Neb and spoke urgently, 'Sir, we need to give them a rest. The stone is unstable – we must secure it –'

He spoke too late. The men had lost control of the rope. Their muscles were too tired to hold on any longer and the massive stone was beginning to slip. They cried out in agony as the rope ripped through their hands, tearing their skin. And the stone moved faster, faster, faster down the slope.

The next few seconds passed in a blur. The stone continued to plummet. The men at the top of the ramp looked down in horror. Meanwhile Ipuy, a young scribe, hurried towards the overseer to deliver a report, his head bent with busy thoughts. He didn't see the stone. The deputy opened his mouth to shout.

'Ipuy!'

Ipuy glanced up at the ramp. It was the last thing he would ever see – the ramp, and the massive block of limestone that was about to snuff out his life. He gave a short, final scream. And then he was dead.

For one instant, silence fell as dust settled and the men stood still in shock. It was the deputy who moved first, hurtling towards the great stone and the young man who lay beneath it. His heart was already bursting with grief.

'No! No, no!' he cried. 'Not Ipuy. Please, please not Ipuy . . .'

But all that could be seen of Ipuy was one leg, jutting out from beneath the stone. There was no hope, no hope at all. The deputy sank to the ground, and clutched that one foot and leg, soaking it in tears. Ipuy had been his best friend.

It was some time before the men could tear him away. But the stone had to be lifted, and the body pulled out. The deputy looked up to see Hat-Neb shouting orders.

'Stop gawping!' he barked. 'Anyone would think you'd never seen a corpse before! Form two lines and start lifting!'

The deputy gazed at him through his watery eyes. *I hate you,* he thought. *You have brought nothing but hardship and misery to me and my men. Now you have killed my best friend. I hate you. And if it's the last thing I do, I will get my revenge.*